Copyright © 2023
All rights reserved
The characters and events portrayed in this book are fictitious. Any similarities to real persons, living or dead, is coincidental and not intended by the author.

No part of this book may be reproduced, or stored in a retrieval system, or transmitted in any form or by any means, electronic, mechanical, photocopying, recording, or otherwise, without express written permission of the author.
Author: Nicholas Grady

Under the Bluffs

by Nicholas Grady

A word about caves in The Twin Cities

If you're not from the area you may not know this, but the cities of Minneapolis and Saint Paul have hidden caves all over the place! Some of them are quite small and only go in 20-100 feet. But others are huge, covering miles of cavernous spaces. The majority of these caves are manmade, and have been used for silica mining, cold storage for breweries, mushroom growing, cheese aging, and a few were even used as night clubs back in the day.

The Ford Motor Company dug out a huge mine for silica which at one time was used to make glass for windshields at the now defunct Ford plant.

There are stories of gangsters hiding out in the caves in the 1920's and 1930's, people dying in them (which has happened on more than one occasion), and there are all sorts of urban legends surrounding them. Most believe that they are haunted as well.

The cities of Saint Paul and Minneapolis have tried over the years to seal these caves off, but being that the majority of them were dug into sandstone bluffs along the Mississippi River, once a cave is sealed off it doesn't take long for an experienced urban explorer to find or dig a new way in. Many of the caves have more than one entrance as well. So the efforts of the cities to seal these caves off permanently has been a more or less futile and usually temporary effort at best.

The majority of the caves were dug out starting in the mid to late 1800's, but several of them still stand today, abandoned. They are dangerous to explore, and more than one person has died in them, usually due to carbon monoxide poisoning which was as a result of a fire that was made in a cave at some point.

The caves are primarily abandoned today, with the exception of the Wabasha Street Caves in Saint Paul, which remain as a local attraction, wedding venue, and night club. Of course, there are always urban explorers who know where the other caves are and find a way into them, and in some cases even hold secret parties or events in these hidden locations. A quick YouTube search of Saint Paul caves will reveal countless visits to these undisclosed locations.

In some cases, people have gotten lost in these caves, or managed to find a way in only to discover that they couldn't get back out and needed to be rescued by the fire department. There has been more than one time that a cave rescue or a party bust has made the local news.

Exploration is not recommended and considered dangerous.

Chapter 1

1983

There were several things that happened in 1983. Some were more significant than others. Michael Jackson's Thriller was released, spent 22 weeks at number one, and sold over 15 million copies. The final episode of the TV series MASH aired and was viewed by 125 million people. The first Mario Brothers game was released, Fraggle Rock premiered on HBO, and Return of the Jedi wowed audiences at the theatre bringing an end to the Star Wars trilogy.

These events were important to some, and to others not so much. But for Detective Ron Clark nothing was more significant than the letter that he received on April 14th, 1983.

There was a snowstorm that day in Saint Paul, Minnesota which was unusual for that time of year. It made road conditions terrible and there were several accidents, which was why Ron more or less found himself alone at his desk in the police station at 4:00 in the afternoon with little to do. Ron was around 6 feet tall, and in reasonable shape for his age.

Most of Ron's fellow officers were out that day helping clear traffic, assisting with fender benders, and helping with other vehicle accidents that were caused by the storm. The station was practically empty.

Ron worked the missing person cases, which often coincided with murders, kidnappings, and suicides. Ron had just finished up some paperwork and was dreading the commute home in the storm. Despite his 38 years of age and driving experience he had found that his purchase of a 1978 rear wheel drive Monte Carlo left something to be desired when it came to driving in the snow. He ran his fingers through his graying brown hair as he looked out the window, watching the snow come down in heaps outside. He sighed in annoyance at the falling snow and decided that he might as well look through his mail before attempting what would more than likely be a long commute home.

Most of the mail was junk; ads, information about the upcoming wounded officers' fundraiser, credit card applications, and so on. But then he came across something peculiar, an envelope addressed to him written in green ink of all things. He opened it to find a very strange and somewhat disturbing note inside. The note read as follows:

Two will disappear, you will not find them.

"Well what the hell is this?" he thought to himself.

This was not the first time that he had received unusual mail. As a somewhat well-known detective in the city Ron had received everything from thank you letters to death threats over the years and he usually just dismissed anything out of the ordinary. But there was something that got under his skin about this one, maybe it was the green ink? He wasn't sure, but he had cause to believe that something bad was going to happen. Unfortunately, with no return address, and no further information, he wasn't really sure what to do about it.

He immediately reached out to the chief and told him about it but much like himself, the chief agreed that there wasn't a whole lot that they could do about it at the time. So Ron kept it as potential evidence, bagged and tagged it, and dropped it off at the evidence locker.

The Park

Sally and Tim Hanson were 10 and 8 years old respectively. They both had light blonde hair and blue eyes. They lived in the Como neighborhood of Saint Paul. On April 14th, 1983 they went to play in the snow at the park near their house after school with the expectation that they would come home by 5:00 for dinner. Back in those days, people weren't as worried about their kids going out on their own. The world was a safer place back then.

Sally had a new digital wristwatch that she had gotten for Christmas so she had no concerns that both she and Tim would be back at home in time for dinner. She checked the watch regularly since it was such a new and unique item to her at the time.

The snow was quite deep and the 6 block hike to the park was somewhat tiring for both children, especially Tim who was quite short for his age. He struggled to drag his feet over the deep, slushy snow and complained several times to Sally that they should just go and play in the back yard at home. Sally explained that they were already past the halfway point and going back home now would just be more trudging through the snow without the reward of being able to play at the park.

When they finally reached the park they had a wonderful time…..throwing snow balls at each other, catching snowflakes on their tongues, and running around on the jungle gyms. They built a snowman together, and had not even noticed the car parked nearby that had been sitting there the entire time with the engine running.

They were being watched, and the person inside the vehicle had plans for them, but they were completely oblivious to this. They were too lost in the joyful bliss of childhood play to worry about the vehicle or even notice it for that matter.

At some point Sally Hanson pulled up the sleeve of her puffy red snowsuit to check the time on her wristwatch and noticed that it was 4:40. It was time to head back home. She signaled to Tim who was on the swing set that it was time to go, and Tim begrudgingly stopped swinging and followed his sister, as he always did.

They began walking towards home and Tim complained again about trudging through the snow and that he was tired. Just then a car (the same car that had been sitting there the whole time) pulled up alongside of them. Sally and Tim looked over at the vehicle as they walked.

The passenger window rolled down and a man said "you kids need a ride home? Looks like the snow is pretty deep?" Sally and Tim stopped.

"We're not supposed to take rides from strangers," said Sally.

The man smiled and said "oh, well I'm no stranger! I live down the block from you two. We're neighbors. My name is Frank. Don't you remember me? I helped your folks clear some snow a few weeks ago with my snow blower."

Sally tried to remember Frank helping out her parents with snow removal but couldn't remember if this had happened or not. Sally's family didn't have a snow blower, so there had been times when neighbors had helped them clear snow, but she didn't recognize Franks face. She guessed it could be possible though?

"C'mon, hop in! It's only a few blocks," said Frank.

Sally thought to herself that only someone that knew where they lived could have known that they were that close to home. So unless he was taking a wild guess, she thought that he probably did know their parents and was a neighbor.

Sally looked at Tim who was tired and cranky at this point, and thought about trudging the 6 long blocks through the snow with him whining and complaining the entire way. She didn't really feel like dealing with that, and she decided that there couldn't be any harm in accepting a ride from a neighbor so both she and Tim hopped in the car. The car slowly pulled away from the park, and headed in the direction of their home. "you guys want some candy?" said Frank.

Sally was going to say no because she thought it would spoil their dinner but before she could say anything, Tim already had a piece of chocolate in his hand and was eating it. Sally figured if Tim was eating it she might as well too and took a piece of candy from Frank.

They were about a block from home. Sally was looking out the window of the car watching the snow fall and she suddenly realized that she was starting to feel very sleepy. Her eyes were getting heavy and she was having trouble keeping them open. She looked over at Tim who was already asleep next to her. What was happening? Why did she feel so tired? Why was Tim asleep? Before she could piece anything together or figure out what was going on she was fast asleep in the backseat.

The car drove past their house but it kept going. As it turns out, Frank was not their neighbor, did not know their parents, and had never helped clear any snow. His name wasn't even Frank for that matter. The car drove on through the deep snow moving along slowly. Sally and Tim would never get home again.

Traffic

At 5:00 PM detective Ron Clark finally called it a day. He said his goodbyes to the few officers that still remained at the station and walked out to the parking lot. His Monte Carlo was covered in snow. He gave a long sigh as he approached his car. He brushed the snow off of the keyhole for the driver side door with his hand, opened it, and grabbed his snow scraper and brush. It was an April snow, and that meant rain and snow mixed, nasty business when clearing one's windshield. Ron brushed off the snow and then spent several minutes scraping off the ice that had built up on his windshield. He hopped in his car, started it up, and waited for it to warm up a bit. He reached into his pocket and pulled out a pack of Camel filters and grabbed one out. He pushed in the cigarette lighter in his car ashtray and waited for it to pop. He then lit his cigarette and rolled down his window halfway.

Ron sat there, enjoying his cigarette, and watching the snowfall as his frigid car slowly warmed up. He couldn't stop thinking about that strange letter written in green ink though. What was that all about? Some kind of threat? A warning? Or maybe just another weirdo sending random crap to the cops just to mess with them? Hopefully it was just another nut job.

A few years back he had received several letters from someone stating that they were going to bomb the station, but nothing ever happened. In the end it turned out to be an elaborate prank staged by a teenager who had been mad about getting a speeding ticket. Ron hoped that this would be a similar situation and that the strange letter written in green ink was just some sort of hoax or a prank.

Ron finished his cigarette, flicked the butt into the snow, and rolled up his window. He started driving out of the parking lot and made it about 20 feet before his tires started spinning in the snow. He was stuck. He cranked the wheel to the right and tried again with no luck, then to the left. He threw it in reverse and did the same thing but again no luck. He looked around but he was more or less the last car in the lot at this point so he'd have to figure something out.

Ron kept a snow shovel in his trunk for such occasions and spent a good 20 minutes digging out his vehicle before he was able to get moving again. This time he was able to get out onto the main road which was a bit easier to drive on. Although the plows hadn't come through yet, the road had been driven on by several cars already which had packed the snow down a bit and made it easier to drive.

By the time Ron got out of the lot it was already 5:30. It wasn't much longer before he was stuck in downtown traffic. Cars were getting stuck all over the place, and on top of this there was more than one fender bender situation going on in the area causing additional delays. It was going to be a long drive home. It took Ron at least 20 minutes just to travel 5 blocks. He was starting to get frustrated.

He looked out of his somewhat fogged up window to see the Gopher Bar on his left with the open sign on, he looked at the traffic ahead and behind of him, and then noticed that there was a parking spot open about 20 feet in front of him. "Yep," he said to himself, and pulled into the spot as soon as he got close enough to do so. He zipped up his jacket, left the warmth of his car which had taken a good 15 minutes to achieve in the first place, and headed into the bar.

Ron went to the Gopher bar a lot. It was conveniently on his way home, had good Coney Island hot dogs, and cheap drinks. The atmosphere left a bit to be desired but hey, you can't have everything can you? Ron went to the Gopher bar so frequently that everyone at the station knew it. It was not uncommon for him to receive phone calls from work when he was there. This night was no different.

Ron walked into the bar around 6:00 PM. He had just enough time to order a Coney Dog, get a shot of Jameson, and take a sip before the bar phone rang.

The bartender answered the phone, and shortly thereafter handed the receiver to Ron. "It's for you," the bartender said.
Ron rolled his eyes and took the receiver knowing that it was more than likely dispatch asking him to do some sort of favor and he wasn't wrong.
"Hello?", said Ron, "Yep……uhuh……..yeah I'm pretty close to Como, I can get there within an hour depending on traffic."
He handed the receiver back to the bartender, slammed the rest of his shot and said "looks like I'll take that Coney dog to go."

Once back in his car the traffic was still moving along at a snail's pace. Ron began thinking about the call he'd received. Dispatch had asked him to check in on a family in the Como neighborhood who were worried about their two children. Apparently the kids went to the park and were supposed to be home by 5PM but never came home. In most cases this was usually just kids not paying attention to the time and 90% of the time the children were found and returned safely to their homes. Of course, for Ron this got him thinking back to the letter…..*Two will disappear, you will not find them*…..could it be possible? Were these the two? Or was this just a complete coincidence. After all people went missing all of the time. In fact, there were usually several missing persons cases every month that Ron dealt with so it might just be nothing. He could only hope that once he reached the home that he could find the children quickly and get them home safely.

The Hanson House

Normally a 10-minute drive or so, it took Ron about 35 minutes to get to the Hanson's house with traffic. He arrived to find two very upset and concerned parents. The Hanson's were your typical upper middle class white parents. The father wore a shirt and tie and the mother looked like something out of an 80's sit com. They told Ron that the kids had gone to the park to play, something that they did all the time. They told him that the kids were usually home on time or close to it, especially since they'd given their daughter a digital wristwatch for Christmas so they were very concerned. Sally always had the watch with her they said, and since she'd gotten it had never been late coming home. The Hanson's said that they'd already driven to the park and back several times, and looked around the neighborhood but hadn't had any luck.

Ron said that he'd look around for them and ask around the neighborhood to see if anyone had seen anything. He would do his best to find them, and hopefully bring them home. Ron drove to the park first to see if they had come back there but there was no sign of them. There was a snowman there that had been freshly made so he was certain that they had been there. Unfortunately, any footprints, tire tracks, or other hints that he might find had been buried in the freshly fallen snow. It wasn't going to be easy to find them unless he got lucky.

Ron asked around the neighborhood to anyone who was home for the next three hours but no one had really seen anything. One person had seen the kids walking towards the park but never saw them come back. Another had seen them at the park building a snowman while walking their dog but hadn't seen them since. No one seemed to know where they were. Ron would have to go back to the family empty handed.

When Ron got back to the Hanson's house he found that only the mother was home. Apparently the father had been driving around the neighborhood looking for the kids as well and was not back yet. Ron reported to the mother that he had been unlucky in his search but would keep trying. He told her that he would have more officers canvas the area once they could get there as the roads were still pretty bad with the weather. He asked the mother for some recent photos that he could use to give to the station as well so that other officers could be on the lookout for the children. In addition, he would report this to local news crews in hopes that they would do a story on the missing children, giving them a larger audience of people who would be aware of the situation and hopefully a better chance of finding them.

      Ron reluctantly left the Hanson house empty handed as the mother sat on the sofa, overcome with tears of sorrow. He immediately went to the police station as well as the local news stations to report the incident and provided photos to help everyone try to find the children. He didn't get home until late that night. By morning the story was all over the news broadcasts and had made it to the front page of both major newspapers in the area. Ron could only hope that tips would start coming in that might lead him to finding the children as they were still missing the following day.

The next day

      Ron arrived at the station early despite his being up very late the night before. He arrived to find several messages and leads on the two missing Hanson children. He followed up on every lead that he had but everything led to a dead end.

      There were several potential things that could have happened to the kids. They could have been kidnapped, killed, they could have run away

16

from home (although not likely), and there was even the possibility that they could have been buried alive by the snow plows.

  A few years back a kid had been playing near the boulevard in his front yard and a snow plow had gone by throwing huge amounts of snow on top of him. The kid was buried before he knew what hit him and the driver never saw him. The kid only survived due to an air pocket in the snow. It took over a day to find him and he was still alive when he was found but just barely. That had been a close one as Ron recalled. But then there was that letter…..*two will disappear, you will not find them……*

  Ron had already sent the letter to the lab to check for fingerprints or anything that might help him find the writer but there was nothing other than the actual handwriting that gave any clues, and even that wasn't very helpful. He had traced the letter through the post office but found that it had been mailed from out of state. Maybe the writer had deliberately driven out of state to mail it? But if that was the case there'd be little chance of finding them. Nothing he seemed to do turned up anything. The police were able to trace the pen ink back to a Bic brand pen, but when Ron looked up how many green Bic pens had been sold in the last few months, the numbers were astounding. It would be like looking for a needle in a haystack. In addition, there was still the possibility that the missing kids and the letter were unrelated. Ron was shooting in the dark on this one and was not entirely sure what to do next.

The days dragged on into weeks, and the weeks dragged on into months with no new evidence related to the missing children. The snow had melted and given way past spring and into summer, and Ron was no closer to solving the case than on the day that the Hanson children had disappeared. The letter didn't turn up any more information or leads, nor did calls that came in to the station…..the story was no longer even in the news.

Occasionally there would be a small write up in the paper but nothing significant. Ron reached out to the family on a regular basis to see how they were doing and kept them updated on the case as much as possible. There were missing signs up all over town with the children's photos, and occasionally someone would call in thinking that they had seen the children, but it always turned out to be misinformation. The police had searched everywhere they could think of but the children were never found.

Ron spent a lot of his evenings drinking as a result. He felt like a failure for not finding the Hanson children, and became obsessed with the case. Despite the fact that he had gotten nowhere with the case he refused to give up on it. This continued on for the better part of a year until the case was finally declared cold and Ron was forced to move on to other cases and put it on the backburner. He never forgot the case though, and the children weighed heavily on his mind forever. He continued to look into the case when he had time to do so, but he had more less given up hope of ever finding the children.

The family was devastated. Not knowing was probably the worst part for them. Not knowing if their children were alive or dead, or what might have happened, or what might be happening to them was all too much to think about. Their lives were never quite the same after that and they never saw their children again.

Another Letter

Two years had passed since the disappearance of the Hanson children. For a time, people were more careful with their children, not allowing them to go anywhere alone for fear of their own children disappearing. But as it is with most things people became less cautious over time and it wasn't long until kids were free to go out on their own again. People had become more complacent about the kidnapping and were no longer concerned about it.

Ron sat at his desk in the station drinking coffee and looking over the most recent missing person's cases on a warm June afternoon. He'd had some luck finding people in the past 2 years, sometimes alive, and sometimes dead. But he still thought about the Hanson kids every day. He even kept their pictures on his desk as a reminder that they were still out there, somewhere, and one day he might actually find them despite the fact that no one besides him had even touched the case in a year.

He looked through his mail and his face turned white when he found a letter addressed to him written in Green ink. Without even thinking about it he tore it open only to find a similar note to the one that he had received on that horrible day in 1983. The note read as follows:

Two more will disappear, you will not find them.

Ron quickly went to his superior to report this. After all, the last time that this had happened two kids had disappeared and were never found. Ron and the rest of the police force did everything that they could to warn the community, contacting local news and setting up a curfew. They kept the letter itself confidential. The news broadcasts called it a "community concern" and requested that parents not let their children go out alone. The reasoning behind this was that Ron didn't want the kidnapper knowing that he knew that there had been a connection between the letters and the kidnappings, not yet anyways. Parents were also told to have their children at home after 7PM.

Despite the efforts of the police force, two children disappeared once again, and once again Ron did his best to find them with no luck.

Over the next 8 years Ron received 3 more letters, and each time two children went missing, never to be found again. In case you've lost count that's 10 children that went missing in total, and each time they were lost forever. Ron had started to believe that they were all dead, but he couldn't be 100% sure. After all, up to this point there hadn't actually been any concrete evidence at all. Not one body had been found. All that Ron knew was that this kept happening, would probably happen again, and despite his efforts there appeared to be nothing that he could do about it. Advances in technology had come along in regards to finding evidence, but still nothing on this kidnapper, murderer, or whatever he or she was. There was no DNA, no vehicle sightings near the locations of the kidnappings, no witnesses, nothing.

    Ron had all but given up. Other detectives had tried and failed as well, even those that later worked on the cold case files dating back to 1983. There were never any fingerprints, and handwriting analysis revealed nothing that could really help find a lead. The letters had been mailed from all different parts of the country, even as far away as Chicago so there was no pattern there either. Ron kept hoping that the next time around he'd catch this person, or at least find the kids, or maybe even a body, but it never happened. Ron could only hope that the letters would stop or that the monster that was doing this would quit at some point.

Chapter 2

1993

In the summer of 1993 Tony and Jeff were having the time of their lives. They had recently graduated from high school (which they both hated), and were just starting to enjoy the freedom of adulthood. Although not entirely independent from their parents yet, they both had jobs and being out of high school was a relief. Neither of them really knew what they were going to do with their lives but they didn't really care at that point. For the time being, they were both content to work their dead end jobs at an auto parts warehouse, skateboard, get high, and listen to as much grunge music as they could get their hands on. They were particularly big fans of Soundgarden, since one of Soundgarden's songs gave a nod to Minnesota, their home state.

You could usually find them skateboarding around Saint Paul, wearing ripped up jeans, rock band t-shirts, and flannel shirts if the weather was cold. Both boys had long, shoulder length brown hair and both of them were kind of skinny. They were practically twins in the way that they dressed and wore their hair. It wasn't uncommon when they were in high school for a teacher or an administrator to mistake one for the other. They both played in a garage band as well, and when they weren't skateboarding, getting high, playing guitar, or working they were out doing what people these days refer to as urban exploring.

Their jobs paid okay, but were painstakingly dull. They basically just showed up at the warehouse and spent their day walking around the warehouse with order sheets and carts, pulling orders off of the shelves for the different stores around the area. It was boring and mindless work.

When they weren't working, they liked to find old abandoned buildings, utility tunnels, and even open sewers to explore. But their true passion was exploring the old abandoned mines and caves that were hidden all over the Twin Cities. At this time, you could usually only find these places by word of mouth, so part of the adventure was finding some of these places or searching for them. There were very few people doing this at the time so the urban exploring community was fairly small.

They'd been caught more than once by the police trying to infiltrate a building or some other location so they had to be careful. The cops knew who they were and didn't particularly like the two of them risking their necks to explore these abandoned places. However, when they did get caught they were usually just given a slap on the wrist, told not to do it again, and sent on their merry way. The local cops knew that the boys were more or less harmless and had better things to do with their time.

On June 23rd, 1993, Tony and Jeff decided to check out a few of the caves that they had visited before and hopefully find some new ones. They met up at their usual spot, a Burger King located near the Mississippi river in Downtown Saint Paul. The Burger King was close to the river bluffs which is where the majority of the caves were located. Although there were caves in other parts of the city, the bluffs were usually where they had the best luck finding a new cave.

Jeff sat on the patio at the Burger King waiting for Tony to arrive. He had his headphones on and was blasting a cassette tape of Alice in Chains. Tony was usually late so Jeff wasn't surprised that he was once again the first to arrive. Jeff reached into his pocket and pulled out a wooden dugout with a pinch hitter inside.

A dugout, in case you didn't know, is a small wooden case used for holding and covering the smell of marijuana. A pinch hitter is a pipe that fits into the dugout and is designed to fit just enough weed to take a hit or two. It resembles a baseball bat in appearance so 'pinch hitter' is a baseball reference as well as a reference to the amount of weed one can fit into the pipe itself (a small pinch). A dugout is just that, a dugout piece of wood that can hold a small amount of marijuana along with a pinch hitter pipe. Anyways, enough about paraphernalia.

Jeff looked around to make sure that no one was watching, opened up the dugout, loaded the pinch hitter and lit it with his lighter, taking a few long puffs before it ran out. He smoked just enough to get a good buzz going. He quickly put the dugout away so as not to be noticed as unlike recent laws in the U.S., weed was still illegal and frowned upon in the community at that time. One could say that it's still frowned upon today, but it's at least more socially acceptable these days.

      Jeff waited for a few minutes and seeing that Tony was not coming up the street began skating around on the patio, practicing Ollies onto the picnic table benches. It wasn't long before the manager, an overweight cranky man with a thick moustache stepped out onto the patio.

"Hey pal," said the manager.

Jeff didn't respond as he couldn't hear the manager with his headphones blasting. The manager crossed his arms, "I SAID HEY PAL!"

Jeff heard him the second time and was startled mid-Ollie causing him to lose his balance and fall onto the patio.

"Ah fuck!" exclaimed Jeff as he fell to the ground, landing on his tailbone. He looked up at the manager who by this point was standing over him. "Bro, you scared the shit outta me! Why are you yelling like that?" said Jeff.

The manager rolled his eyes and said, "I yelled at you because you didn't respond on account of blasting music when I tried to get your attention the first time, you idiot!"

Jeff stood up and brushed himself off. "Oh, my fault," said Jeff. "What's up?"

"You can't just loiter on the patio here getting stoned and skateboarding. You either gotta buy something or you gotta go," said the manager.
Jeff looked annoyed. "Okay, well my buddy is meeting me here in a few minutes and then I'll leave okay?"
The manager nodded, rolled his eyes again and went back inside.
"Prick," Jeff mumbled to himself.
      A few moments later Jeff looked down the road to see the silhouette of a tall, lanky, long haired body skateboarding up the street. The heat of the sun and the effect of the marijuana distorted his view but Jeff knew who it was. "About time," he mumbled to himself.
Tony skated up to the patio, kicked up his board into his hand and smiled.
"Sorry I'm late," said Tony.
 "You're always late, I've grown to expect it," said Jeff.
"You at least bring everything?" said Jeff.
 Tony pulled off a backpack from his shoulders and unzipped it to reveal 2 high powered flashlights, 2 bottles of water, a 20-foot length of rope, and a Ziploc bag with some very potent weed inside of it. Tony smiled.
"This ought to do it!" said Tony.
 Jeff smiled, "Looks like you managed to get to your dealer?" said Jeff, pointing to Tony's bag of weed.
"Duh!" exclaimed Tony, "Why do you think I was late? Fucker wasn't there when he said he would be and I had to wait around for 20 minutes!"

Jeff looked at Tony and said "Well, as long as you're sharing I guess I can forgive your tardiness."

"Of course! Who better to share it with!" said Tony. "C'mon Jeff, days a wastin'! Let's go!"

"Sounds good," said Jeff.

Tony closed up the backpack, hopped on his skateboard, and headed toward the long downhill bridge that crossed the river towards the bluffs. Jeff was right behind him. The two flew down the bridge on their skateboards at a somewhat dangerous pace, hoping that the stoplight at the end of the bridge would be green when they crossed the road to the parkway. If it wasn't they'd run the risk of crossing the road into oncoming traffic and wouldn't be able to stop.

If you've never ridden a skateboard at high speed downhill it can be quite dangerous. The slightest movement could lead to something known as the speed wobbles. Basically what happens is your board starts wobbling under your feet causing it to wiggle across the ground left and right until you eventually lose your balance and fall off of it. It usually doesn't end well. Fortunately, Tony and Jeff had ridden down this hill enough times to get very good at it and they sailed down the hill without any issue. As they were approaching the stoplight at the bottom of the hill, the don't walk light was flashing, indicating that the light would turn red soon. Luckily for them they got through the light just in time and as the landscape leveled out in front of them at the bottom of the hill they gradually slowed down to a safer and saner speed.

They turned onto the parkway a few blocks down which ran along the bluffs and started looking for trails or breaks in the foliage that might lead up to a new cave or one that they had already visited in the bluffs before. The caves were scattered along the bluffs and the ways to get into them were usually quite treacherous. Some of them had openings no bigger than a foot or 2 wide. There were even some that were so small that it required one to army crawl in order to get in. Some of the caves were located close to the parkway at ground level, while others required climbs up the bluffs for hundreds of feet before reaching an entrance.

The bluffs themselves were treacherous in their own right. They were covered with loose sand, gravel, and rocks that could lead to a landslide. One wrong step while climbing could lead to a painful or even deadly fall. From the parkway road the bluffs stretched up hundreds if not thousands of feet. On a previous adventure the boys had climbed up 500 feet or so to find a cave entrance that they had been told about. About 10 feet from the entrance Jeff had slipped on some loose rocks and had he not managed to grab a tree root would have certainly fallen to his death.

As they rode their boards along the parkway Tony noticed a squad car heading in their direction from the other end of the parkway. He could only hope that it was a rookie who had yet to get to know the two of them. If it was a local cop that already knew them, they might be in trouble. Both of them were carrying weed, and the rest of the contents in the backpack would surely lead to another lecture about the dangers of urban exploring if it was searched.

As they got closer Tony stopped to see who was driving the squad car. Jeff caught up to him and stopped as well. The squad car began slowing down on its approach and the boys looked to see an African American cop with a shaved head and a beard pull over across the street from them. The officer looked over at them and smiled. The boys looked at each other and simultaneously said "Wallace" with a groan.

Officer Wallace stepped out of the car and waved to the boys as he ambled across the street. Wallace was 6' 3", very well built, and not someone to mess with. The boys knew him well as he had caught them sneaking out of a cave a few months back, as well as caught them a few times in other places while exploring.

"Well hello boys!" said officer Wallace with a joyous yet condescending tone. "How we doin' today?"

"Fine," the boys said disappointingly.

"What are ya up to today then boys?" said officer Wallace in the same tone.

Jeff piped in "just skating over to our friend Tommy's house."

"Is that right?" said officer Wallace.

"Yes sir!" said Tony.

"And where exactly does Tommy live?" asked Wallace.

"Just on the other side of the park." replied Jeff, pointing up the road.

"Well it seems to be pretty hot outside today? How's about I give you a ride?" Wallace said.

"Oh….umm that's ok. We kinda wanna skate there," Said Tony.

"Boys? Get in the car," said Wallace.

The two looked at each other, terrified. But they didn't really have any choice. They reluctantly followed officer Wallace to his car and got in the back seat, hoping that he wouldn't smell the weed on them or search the backpack. If he did, they could be faced with marijuana possession charges or at the very least Wallace could confiscate it just to be a prick. Officer Wallace turned the car around and headed down the parkway in the direction that he had come from.

"So whose house are we going to again?" Wallace asked, knowing that the boys were lying.

"Tommy's," Jeff said, "it's just up the hill past the marina on the other side of the park."

"Uh-huh," Wallace said, "well I'll tell ya what boys, you may know a kid named Tommy, and he may live on the other side of the marina, but I know bullshit when I hear it so here's what's gonna happen. I'm gonna talk to you boys for a bit while I drive you just as far away from those bluffs as I feel is needed so that you don't go back into those damned caves! Understood?"

"Yes sir," Tony said sadly.

"Okay then," Wallace said as he drove on, "now that we understand each other we can move forward. Now I know for a fact that you two knuckleheads are only down around this area when you're looking to find a cave. So I know this story about Tommy is bullshit. I also know that people have gotten injured, trapped, as well as died in those caves! Hell, you could die of Carbon Monoxide poisoning, a ceiling could collapse on ya, who knows? So I'm not about to let you two go in there and die on my watch...."

Officer Wallace continued to lecture the boys for another 20 minutes or so until they were miles away from the caves. He dropped them off at a bus stop on the other side of town. The boys got out of the car and stood at the bus stop. Wallace looked at them from the inside of the squad car and said "Two things. 1. If I catch you anywhere you aren't supposed to be again I'm gonna cite you for trespassing. 2. If I catch you holding weed again I'm gonna bust you for that as well......and don't tell me you're not holding, you two reeked like stale bong water and skunks the second you got into my car. Have a good day boys!" Officer Wallace waved to the boys and drove off.

What Wallace didn't realize, was that he had dropped the boys off at a bus stop whose route literally took them right back to where they had started in the first place, the Burger King. The two looked at each other and smiled.
"You got money for bus fare?" asked Tony.
"I sure do!" replied Jeff.

The two laughed and waited for the bus, knowing that they could get back to the caves in 20 minutes or so, and that the chances of Wallace coming by again was highly unlikely.

It was not long before the boys were back skating along the parkway, right where they had left off. Their detour (courtesy of officer Wallace) had not deterred them on their mission for that day. This time around there were no squad cars in sight and the traffic on the road was minimal. The coast was more or less clear.

As they skated along the parkway Jeff noticed an opening in the foliage on the other side of the road that he hadn't seen before. He stopped skating and signaled to Tony who was a few feet ahead of him. The two looked across the road and noticed a narrow winding trail going up the hill into the bluffs. "Have we been up this one before?" asked Tony.

"I don't think so," said Jeff.

The two looked around to see if anyone was coming up the road or the walking path. Jeff listened for traffic and heard nothing. "GO!", said Jeff and the two sprinted across the street and disappeared behind the brush and foliage that made the path nearly impossible to see from the road unless you were looking for it. Once behind the first set of trees and bushes the boys stopped for a moment and looked back, just to make sure that no one had seen them. It appeared to them that they were safely across the road and into the woods.

They looked ahead of them to see a steep trail that winded up into the bluffs. It was going to be a challenging climb to find this cave, if there was even anything there. There was silica sand or what in some cases is called sugar sand along the trail. This was usually a good sign that there was a cave due to the fact that other explorers would have tracked sand out of the cave or displaced sand while digging out an entrance if the cave had been sealed off by the city. The boys left their skateboards under some bushes at the base of the bluff, knowing that they'd need the use of both hands to climb up the trail, and began heading up the steep trail.

Climbing up a bluff may seem like a simple task but there is definitely some skill required. One has to have decent foot wear, a fair amount of overall body strength, and a knack for finding footholds, tree roots, and ledges to grab onto in order to avoid slipping or falling. The bluffs along the Mississippi in Saint Paul are generally covered with loose shale rocks and sand due to erosion, so it's easy to slip or slide down from a spot unexpectedly. They are also quite steep. One needs to be prepared for this, and remember where the previous foot hold or hand hold was in order to stop themselves from slipping further or even falling due to these unexpected slips and slides. If one begins to slide backwards due to loose footing, one must grab onto the previous hand hold or slide down to the previous foot hold to stop from falling. There is also always the chance of an unexpected landslide, which has claimed the lives of people more than once over the years. So, in short, it's fairly dangerous.

Tony and Jeff were fairly experienced bluff climbers and had been doing it for years, but this climb was more treacherous than some that they had done before. Tony went first, and Jeff waited at the base of the bluff until Tony could get to a safe place to stop and rest. The reason for this was so that if Tony kicked any rocks loose they wouldn't fall on top of Jeff.

After a few moments Tony whistled from somewhere up the bluff. He was so far up that Jeff couldn't even see him. Jeff began the ascent, being careful to test a tree or root by pulling on it to make sure it was stable before using it as a hand hold. The trail was steep, almost vertical at times. Jeff sort of leap frogged his way up, zigzagging to areas that were more level or provided a ledge until he could move up to the next spot. He pulled himself up by small tress, roots, and rock ledges that he came across along the way. He slipped once, but already had his hand on a strong tree root so there was no fear of falling. By the time he reached Tony they were about 150 feet up the bluff. Tony was standing on a rock ledge about 2 feet wide that stuck out from the bluff. Jeff turned and looked down, it was quite a substantial drop back down to the parkway below.

    The two took a minute to look around further up the bluff to see if there were any signs of a cave opening. Tony noticed some graffiti on the bluff to the right and about 30 feet further up. This was usually a sign that someone had been there and that there might be something to see, so the two climbed up towards the graffiti, hoping that there might be a cave entrance there. They weren't disappointed.

    When they climbed up the last 30 feet, they came upon a small shelf of rock that was covered with sand. It was about 4 feet by four feet wide, and the surrounding rock wall was covered with typical graffiti. Marijuana leaves, random penises, names, gang tags, and satanic symbols covered the small wall. There was even a warning, 'too risky' written above the entrance to the cave.

When most people think about entrances to a cave they usually picture a large opening that can be walked into or at the very least crawled into. This wasn't always the case with caves in Saint Paul. Many of them had been abandoned at least 50 years ago allowing for erosion to fill in the entrances with sand and dirt. In some cases, entrances had collapsed or even half collapsed. In other cases, the city had tried to haphazardly fill them in with dirt or other debris.

Needless to say the entrance to this particular cave that Tony and Jeff had stumbled upon was quite small. In addition to that, it wasn't even a level entrance. The entrance went downhill at about a 45-degree angle. Jeff squatted down to take a closer look. "Hand me one of those flashlights," he said to Tony.

Tony complied. Jeff turned on the flashlight and aimed the light down the narrow hole that was no bigger than 20 inches in diameter. He could feel the cool cave air coming from the hole and on a hot summer day it felt like air conditioning.

"It looks like it opens up about 15 feet in, but we're going to have to slither through the first part here," said Jeff.

Tony, who was already packing up his pipe with weed gave a big thumbs up to Jeff. The two took a few moments to smoke, and then reassessed the entrance.

They decided to use the rope that they had brought along and tied it to a nearby tree, that way they could pull themselves back out when leaving if it seemed too steep. They knew well enough that

more than once people had found their way into caves but gotten stuck trying to get out. Jeff was honestly more worried about getting stuck on the way in…..the only safe way would be to go in feet first. That way he could pull on the rope to snake his way out if he got stuck. If he went in head first he would have to push back on the rope which would be considerably harder. Jeff looked at Tony,
"feet first I'm thinking," said Jeff.
"Yep, no way I'm getting stuck head first and dying while blood rushes to my brain!" said Tony.
Jeff went in first.

  He slowly lowered himself into the hole in such a manner that he was facing toward the bluff, his back was against the ceiling of the entrance, and his knees were against the floor of the cave.

  As he crawled in he felt the cool air that emanated from the cave. Caves in general stay cooler than the outside air in the summer, usually around 50 degrees Fahrenheit. They also have a particular smell. Stale air and an almost moldy or wet smell. This smell gets in your clothes as well and remains for some time.

  Jeff crawled in to just above his chest level and stopped. At this point his arms were in front of him and he quickly realized that if he went any further he'd be stuck with his arms pinned against his chest. He pulled himself out a few feet and then began lowering himself back in, this time with his arms above his head. Fortunately, with the 45-degree angle, gravity worked in his favor and he more or less just had to lower himself in using the rope. About 15 feet down the entrance opened up

to a small room that was about 2 feet wide and around 4 feet high. Still a bit tight but not as claustrophobic as the initial climb in.
"Okay Tony I'm in! It's not that bad but come in with your arms above your head! It opens up after about 15 feet!" yelled Jeff.
"Gotcha!" yelled back Tony.

Tony began climbing in in the same manner as Jeff, taking note to keep his arms above his head, but while lowering himself into the hole he slipped for a moment in one of the tighter spots and found himself stuck. He had accidentally bent his knee while slipping and now his lower leg was wedged with his knee pressed against one side of the hole and his foot the other. He tried to get himself loose by pulling on the rope but was unsuccessful.
"Aghhh! Fuck me!" Jeff heard Tony yell from above as he sat waiting for him.
"You okay?" Jeff yelled back.
"Not exactly!" replied Tony, "I got my leg wedged here. I'm stuck and I can't pull myself back up! You're gonna have to climb up here and pull my foot loose!"

Jeff flashed his light up the narrow hole and could see Tony about 8 feet up.
"God dammit," mumbled Jeff to himself. He grabbed onto the rope and started pulling himself back up until he was close enough to reach Tony's foot. "Don't worry, I got this!" said Jeff. He reached up and grabbed Tony's foot by the back of his shoe and began to pull. Luckily due to the sandstone wall of the hole which crumbled away easily it didn't take long before he got Tony's foot was loose and they

were both able to get back down into the small room.

Once Tony was inside the room with Jeff he looked around.

"Is this it?" said Tony.

"Nope!" said Jeff flashing his light to a corner of the small room where a small tunnel led off to another part of the cave.

Tony smiled and said "NICE!" with enthusiasm.

    The two entered the small tunnel with flashlights in hand. The tunnel was about two feet wide and three feet high. Fortunately for them the climb was not as steep as the entrance and they were able to crawl in on all fours, slowly going down further into the abyss. Without flashlights they would have been in complete darkness at this point. Even the little room that they had just left was barely illuminated by the light from the entrance.

    The tunnel went on for about 50 feet. Jeff was in front with Tony just behind him. Occasionally Jeff's back would scrape the ceiling of the tunnel causing a small shower of sandstone particles to fall onto his head. The cave had clearly not been entered in a very long time as there were spider webs that he had to keep brushing off of his face as they moved along. He could only hope that they'd reach a larger space at some point. Along the walls there were remnants of visitors past. Carved initials in the sandstone, graffiti, and empty beer cans could be seen all over the small tunnel. At the end of the tunnel Jeff could see that it opened up into a much larger space, but he could also see that at the end of the tunnel there was no floor to be seen. Upon reaching the end of the tunnel he stopped as the tunnel came to a ledge that dropped off. Jeff scanned his light into the darkness below. He could see that the tunnel opened up into a huge space with ceilings that were nearly 30 feet high. He could see a main passage that had several offshoots and became very excited. The cave was vast and there would be plenty to explore. Unfortunately, when he scanned his light downward from the mouth of the tunnel he noted that it was about a twelve-foot drop to the floor of the cave. Easy enough to hop into, but too high to climb out of.

He looked down along the wall in front of him below the tunnel and noted that there were some foot holds dug into the sandstone leading up to the tunnel that had been made by previous visitors. He also noticed a board on the floor that was around 7 feet long. Between the footholds and the board he figured that they could get back out without an issue.

At this point Tony caught up to Jeff and got a look out of the end of the tunnel at the huge cavernous space ahead of them.
"Holy Shit dude! This is huge!" exclaimed Tony.
At this point they were crouched next to each other at the end of the tunnel, scanning the space with their flashlights.
"There's some footholds dug into the sandstone down there, and I saw a board that we could lean against the wall to climb back up as well if needed. Do you think we can get back out?" asked Jeff.
Tony flashed his light down to see what Jeff was talking about. He saw the old footholds dug into the

sandstone wall sort of like a makeshift ladder, and also noticed the board on the ground below. "Oh...hell yeah dude, we can totally get back up that!" said Tony, who was already getting ready to drop in to the cave. Tony went down feet first facing the tunnel so that he could hang from the ledge and drop down. It was fairly easy to do and Jeff immediately followed his lead.

    Once on the floor of the cave the boys took a few moments to look around and get their bearings before going further. They knew from previous experiences that it was easy to get lost in some of the bigger caves and that making mental notes of landmarks along the way was always a good idea. In some of the bigger caves they had brought along long rolls of sturdy string and literally unrolled it as they went, eventually following the string back to where they had started so that they wouldn't get lost. They probably should have brought some string on this day but had no idea that they were going to find a cave this large.

    The room that they dropped into was massive. The Ceilings were more than 30 feet high, and the room itself was at least 200 feet in diameter. There were at least 4 tunnels leading off from it, all around 12 feet high and 10 feet wide. The ceiling in the room was sort of a giant dome, and the tunnels leading from the room had ceilings that gradually formed into a point sort of like the roof of a house. The walls of the room were covered with sandstone carvings and graffiti. Mostly names of people who had been there before, initials and such. There were band logos carved or spray painted along the walls as well. Mostly bands from the 70's and 80's......Led Zeppelin, Pink Floyd, Metallica, Van Halen, and so on. There was scarcely a section of the walls that didn't have something spray painted or carved on them making the cave walls a sort of collage of graffiti and carvings. The floors were made of typical silica sand, a very soft and fine grained sand that felt like the sand one walks upon when on an ocean beach. It was almost squishy to walk on. The floor of the cave was littered with the refuse of past parties. There were old beer cans, broken glass, empty booze bottles, all kinds of junk. Some of the beer cans were so old that they more resembled a soup can and had the old style pull off tab openings on the top.

"Dude, this has gotta be one of the biggest ones we have ever seen! I'm counting at least 4 tunnels going from this room. I'd bet this one's an old mine.....maybe used by the brick company back in the day or for glass with all the silica.....," said Jeff.

"Yeah it's too big to be a brewery cave, but it's definitely man made. My guess is that you used to be able to enter it closer to ground level but the original entrance must have collapsed or gotten sealed off at some point. I'd say that someone found a ventilation shaft up the bluff and dug it out....that's how we got in," said Tony.

Tony aimed his light at one of the passages that was more or less heading in the same direction as the tunnel that they had just come through.

"See that one? I bet that leads to the original entrance," said Tony.

"Yep, probably right. Let's check that one first. We might find an easier way out as well," said Jeff.

Tony and Jeff walked into the passage which more or less led underneath the tunnel that they had just come through and went back in the direction of the parkway. Of course unlike the way that they had gotten in this was more or less level ground, 15 feet wide or so, and had ceilings that were much taller than either boy, allowing them to walk upright and comfortably. If this passage led to another entrance they might be able to avoid climbing back up through the tiny tunnels and then down the steep bluff that had led them there in the first place, making for a much easier exit. Again much like the rest of the cave the walls were covered with all kinds of carvings and graffiti. There were even a few 3 dimensional carvings of demonic looking faces. The passage went on for about 150 feet and dead ended at a wall made of cinder block and cement. The entrance had clearly been sealed off by the city at some point. The boys could see a little bit of light coming in from the top of the wall but it was too high to get to the top of and appeared to be too small to crawl through as well so the boys were out of luck and would probably have to go out the way that they had come in.

They headed back and started exploring the other passages. Some of them were similar to the first one that they had just explored in that they just led to dead ends, but a few led to other large rooms in the cave, and little side tunnels that one could crawl through to find other rooms within the cave. They found a few tunnels similar to the one that they had come in through that headed upwards as well but they all led to dead ends.

The final passage that they entered was a bit larger than the others, about 25 feet wide and equally as tall. As they wandered down the passage there were several other tunnels that led to other rooms that had clearly been used for partying back in the day due to all of the garbage in them and the faint smell of urine.

This final passage was very deep and went back at least 500 feet. As they got closer to the end of it they could hear the sound of running water. Jeff also heard a strange noise for a brief moment over the sound of the water. It almost sounded like a child crying quietly. It spooked him for a moment but then he told himself that he was stoned and probably just hearing things over the sound of the water. They came to the end of the passage to find a large open space with what appeared to be an underground lake, about 50 feet across and easily 100 feet wide. There was a pipe sticking through the wall of the cave in one area that had water pouring out of it, thus being the source of water for the lake. It appeared that the water had eroded the sandstone in this room, perhaps being the creator of this gigantic space. They walked to the edge of the lake and scanned over the area with their flashlights. Tony picked up a large rock that was by the edge of the lake and heaved it into the water to test the depth.

The rock struck the water with a loud thud that echoed and resonated through the cave for several seconds. The rock sunk into the lake, but was

still visible from the bottom. The water was at most 3 feet deep. As the rock sunk Tony noticed something move in the water.
"What was that?" he asked Jeff.
Jeff wasn't entirely sure.
"Only one way to find out!" said Jeff, and he began walking into the water toward where the rock had landed. Tony stayed on the shore, not willing to get himself soaked over what was probably nothing.

As Jeff approached where the rock had landed he noticed something red in color near the rock. As he got closer he began to realize what it was. It appeared to be a children's snow suit, just big enough for a child who was maybe 8 or 10 years old. When he got close enough he reached for it to pull it out if the water.
"What is it?" Tony asked.
"Just some old clothing or some shit I think," said Jeff.
Jeff grabbed the snow suit and pulled on it. As he pulled on it he flipped it over and suddenly let out a startled yelp.
"What is it?" asked Tony with curiosity.
"It's a fucking dead body! A kid! It's a fucking dead kid!" yelled Jeff.
Jeff immediately dropped the body back into the water and began heading back to the shore of the lake as quickly as he could and then ran past Tony and down the passage towards where they had come in.
"Where you going?" asked Tony.
"The hell outta here that's where I'm going!" yelled Jeff as he ran back towards the entrance of the cave.

Tony looked over at the body that was slowly sinking back into the water. "Yeah man, fuck this," Tony said as he turned and started running as well, catching up to Jeff within a few seconds.

The two of them got back to the main room of the cave, panting and sweating. Years of marijuana use had done some damage to their lungs so they were both always out of breath after sprinting despite riding skateboards on a daily basis. Once they'd had a chance to catch their breath Jeff began repeating to himself "what the fuck, what the fuck, what the serious fuck….." and pacing back and forth in the room. He was full of adrenaline from the scare that the body had given him. All he could see in his mind over and over was the snowsuit turning over to reveal a human skull minus the jawbone which was either somewhere in the snow suit or lost in the murky waters below. "What the fuck….what the fuck!" he kept saying over and over.

Tony quickly realized that Jeff was in a state of shock and handed him a water bottle from his backpack. "Here," Tony said, "drink this."

Jeff took the water bottle from Tony and took a swig. He slowly began calming down. "Dude what the fuck," said Jeff.

"How did that body get down here?" Jeff asked.

"I don't know. Are you sure it was real and not some leftover from a Halloween party or something?" said Tony.

"I am 99% sure it was fucking real dude," replied Jeff, still fighting to catch his breath as he sipped the water.

"That is seriously fucked up. Let's get out of here and then we can figure out what we should do," said Tony.

"Good idea," said Jeff.

The two boys attempted to climb back up to the tunnel from which they had entered using the foot holds that they had seen in the sandstone wall below, but the footholds were too slippery to climb on being covered with loose sand. Tony grabbed the wooden board and leaned it against the wall. He began to walk up the board in a crouched position, holding onto the board with his hands and slowly shimmying up it with his feet. Unfortunately, the piece of wood was old and somewhat rotted and just when he was about to reach the edge of the entrance tunnel the board snapped in half and he fell to the ground with a thud. Luckily the soft sand floor of the cave broke his fall and he wasn't injured, but the boys would have to find another way to get up to the tunnel.

They talked for a few moments and decided to attempt boosting each other up to it. The idea was for Jeff to boost Tony up to the tunnel and then Tony could help pull Jeff out as well. Tony was taller so it made sense for him to go first since he had a longer reach than Jeff. Jeff made a sling with his arms and boosted Tony up as high as he could. Tony was just tall enough to wrap his fingertips around the edge of the little tunnel where they had entered and managed to pull himself the rest of the way up by using the footholds as best he could. His feet slipped out of them several times but he eventually got up to the mouth of the tunnel. Once up there he instructed Jeff to throw up the backpack and his flashlight.

Tony laid on his stomach and reached out his hand as far down as he could so that Jeff might be able to get a running start and jump up to his waiting hand. Jeff tried a running jump several times but was still about a foot short of reaching Tony.
"Try using one of the lower footholds to push off of," said Tony. Jeff gave it one more go, running towards the wall as fast as he could. Jeff was able to jump up and push off of one of the footholds just before his foot slipped out of it, giving him just enough height to reach Tony's hand and grab it. Tony pulled with all his strength as Jeff tried to climb up, Jeff's feet catching the footholds but continuously slipping out of them. It wasn't easy but somehow Jeff got back up there with the help of Tony.
"Next time," Jeff said, "we bring more rope."

The two began the long climb back up the tunnel and were able to pull themselves out by the rope that they had used to get in once they got back to the tiny hole of an entrance. They scrambled down the bluff sliding on their hind sides when needed in order to get away from the cave as quickly as possible.

They grabbed their skateboards at the base of the bluff, checked at the edge of the road for traffic or people walking by, and skated back towards downtown. They stopped into the Burger King to regroup and each ordered a soda so as not to have to deal with the annoying manager giving them crap for loitering.

They sat down at a table on the patio and began to discuss what they should do about their terrifying find in the cave. Tony took a sip of his soda and looked at Jeff in a serious manner and said "this is seriously messed up man. What do you think we should do?"

Jeff looked up at Tony, still a bit shaken by the whole experience and said "we gotta tell the cops one way or another. This kid has probably been missing for who knows how long. But I'm not about to be the one to get involved. We got enough trouble with the cops already."

Tony agreed. "How about an anonymous tip? We could call from a payphone and tell them where to look?" said Tony. "Not a bad idea," replied Jeff, "but we gotta do it somewhere where they won't trace it back to us. If they figure out it's us Wallace is gonna have our asses in a sling!"

The boys decided to get as far away from their usual hangouts as possible before making the call. They skated over to the University of Minnesota Campus and made the call from a payphone located inside one of the student dormitories, hoping that the cops would think it was a college kid making the call and not trace it back to the two of them. They reported where the body was found and gave an approximate location of the cave, hoping that would be enough to point the cops in the right direction. After the events of the day, Tony and Jeff decided that it would be a while before they explored any new caves. The thought of stumbling across another body, getting caught, or getting trapped in a cave was enough for them to stay away for a while.

Chapter 3

Ron Clark sat at his desk at the station, looking over the latest missing person cases. He opened his desk drawer to look for a pen and noticed a picture in the bottom under some post it notes and other junk. He pulled out the picture which was of Sally and Tim Hanson. He sighed and thought to himself "Where are you? Where are all of you?" 10 children had gone missing over the past 10 years, always 2 at a time, and usually around 2 years apart. He had never found a solid lead on any of the cases nor had anyone else. This had driven him into a deep depression, and it affected his life on many levels. He drank too much, had no wife or family, and was more or less a loser in his own mind. Even the cops at the station worried about his wellbeing. Ron popped anti-depressants like they were candy but it didn't really help. At the moment his head was throbbing, the result of drinking more vodka than any human should consume in one sitting the night before.
Officer Wallace approached Ron's desk. "Hey Ron, how's it going?" said Wallace.

"Oh, you know, same shit different day," replied Ron.
"Well I heard about a tip that you might be interested in," said Wallace.
Wallace continued, "someone called in an anonymous tip to the station about an hour ago. They said that they found a kid's body in an abandoned cave up in the bluffs somewhere. I don't know how we're going to get in there because based on the description it sounds impossible to get to but it might be a lead on one of your missing kids." Wallace continued to tell Ron about the call, and how the child had been found wearing a red snowsuit. Ron immediately thought to himself that this could be Sally Hanson. Tim's body could be there as well. They might even find the bodies of some of the other missing children.

After talking to Wallace Ron called the chief and was given the green light to reopen all of the missing children cases that might pertain to the mysterious letters that Ron had received over the years. After all these years he had finally gotten a lead worth investigating.

Although it might lead to nothing, for the first time in ten years Ron finally had a glimmer of hope. He might be able to find the children, and might even be able to finally catch the son of a bitch who was doing this.

He wasted no time. The first call he made was to the rescue squad at the fire department. The rescue squad was a small group of firemen whose specific task was to assist people in danger and in need of help. They had specific tools and equipment required for such scenarios. The rescue squad, in addition to doing regular paramedic work, were also the team that went in to find people after catastrophes such as building collapses, tornadoes, landslides, floods, and they also did their fair share of cave rescues when people found themselves trapped inside of local caves. They were also responsible for sealing off cave entrances when they found them, so they had a good knowledge of some of the cave locations in the area. Ron figured that this would be the crew that could help him get into the cave and find what he hoped to be Sally's body.

Ron told Hank Grady, head of the squad about the situation over the phone. He described the cave location as best he could to Hank. As they talked, Hank looked over old maps of the caves that he had on file and was able to locate what he thought was more than likely the cave that Ron was describing based on the anonymous tip. He told Ron that in order to get in there they would need to dig into the base of the bluff, and then jackhammer through the wall that had been put up when the cave was sealed off years ago. This was the same wall that Tony and Jeff had come across while exploring the cave earlier that day. Hank was somewhat surprised that someone had even gotten into that particular cave as it had been sealed since 1987 as far as he knew. Someone had to have found an entrance somewhere else that must have taken months or even years to dig out in order to get in there.

The rescue squad got to work almost immediately. Ron headed down to the area where the cave was located so that he could get in there just as soon as they got it open. Hank Grady was also on the scene to supervise the excavation. It took the squad a few hours to get the cave open. They had to first dig out the dirt which had spilled down the bluff in front of the entrance over the years using a bobcat until they could reach the cinder block wall that had been put up in 1987 to block the entrance. After that they had to take jackhammers to the wall itself in order to create an opening big enough to walk through. Once it was open Hank provided Ron with some safety equipment: a hard hat, a flashlight, and a personal gas detector that measured oxygen levels as well as methane and carbon monoxide.

    In order to prevent contaminating what would most likely be a crime scene, Hank and Ron were the only ones allowed in once the cave was open. They didn't know exactly where to look but knew that they were looking for an underground lake where the body was supposedly located.

    They entered the cave to see what Tony and Jeff had just seen earlier, a vast cavernous system with graffiti and carvings all over the walls. Ron noted a smell of stale air, almost moldy. The temperature in the cave was significantly cooler than that of the summer weather outside though and in a way it was refreshing.

"It smells odd in here," said Ron.

"Yep, it's your typical cave smell. If you don't wash your clothes that smell can even linger," said Hank.

    They entered into the main chamber, the same space that Tony and Jeff had been in earlier that day. Hank scanned the space with his flashlight

and noticed the small tunnel that Tony and Jeff had dropped out of earlier that day. He noticed that there was recently displaced sand and that the footholds below the tunnel had recently been used.
 "See that?" Hank said as he pointed his light towards the tunnel, "I bet that's how they got in. They must have climbed up the bluff and found a way in above. I wonder how the hell they got back out?"
Ron noticed a broken board on the floor of the cave. "maybe they used this?" Ron said as he pointed his light on the board.
"Yeah, maybe?" said Hank, "The kids who do this stuff are crazy, They're like mice squeezing into spaces that are way too small for the average person. But I kinda get it. These caves are pretty amazing places to explore. I've been in 5 or 6 of them myself but never this one. I'm glad I finally get to have a look inside this one, even if it's for unfortunate reasons." Ron nodded and they moved on, deeper into the cave.
      They wandered around for an hour or so, getting lost a few times before finally stumbling across the lake that Tony and Jeff had described. Upon scanning his light over the top of the water, Ron was able to make out a red blur under the water about 20 feet in. This had to be her, he thought. He carefully walked into the water towards the body, being careful to disturb the scene as little as possible. As he got closer he was almost certain that it was Sally. The snowsuit matched the description that the Hanson family had given him all those years ago. He aimed his light into the water without

moving the body. He could see something in the water reflecting the light back at him next to the body as well. It was fairly small. He reached in and pulled it out to see what it was. After taking a moment to clear off the muck that covered the object he realized what it was and his heart sunk. It was a digital watch. Without knowing anything more he could not be 100% sure, but there was a very good chance that this was Sally Hanson's body.
Hank stood on the shore of the underground lake watching Ron.
"Is it a body?" Hank asked as he wiped the sweat from his brow.
Hank was a larger man, a bit on the hefty side…..not ridiculously overweight but he'd definitely been in better shape in his younger years.
 "I'm pretty sure it's Sally Hanson based on what I remember," said Ron.
"That girl that disappeared with her brother back in the early 80's?" said Hank.
"Yep," said Ron, "without giving too much information, the case of she and her brother ties to several other cases. This might help us finally figure out what's been going on all these years."
	Ron aimed his light over the water slowly and methodically, knowing that if this turned out to be Sally Hanson that there was a good chance that Tim Hanson's body was more than likely somewhere nearby. It was difficult to see through the murky water. Ron could just make out the bottom of the shallow lake about 10 feet in front of him. It appeared that it was no deeper than about three feet. He noticed the pipe sticking out of the cave

wall that was the source of the water pouring into the cave and wondered if someone had broken it on purpose to hide the evidence? He made a mental note to come back and have it checked for DNA and fingerprints.

He left Sally's body where it was, moving slowly through the water in an attempt to see if he could find anything else. About 30 feet away from Sally's body he noticed an unusual object at the bottom of the lake. Without even getting very close he could tell that it was another body, slightly smaller than the first and also wearing outdoor winter clothing. "Tim," he said quietly to himself.

Without knowing what had come over him Ron Suddenly found himself crying. It had been ten long years since the Hanson kids had gone missing, and so many others had followed them. Finally finding them was overwhelming for Ron and he could hardly take it. He managed to compose himself before returning to shore where Hank awaited him.

"Hank, we gotta seal this off as a crime scene," said Ron. "We'll have to put up some police tape, and have regular patrols come through until we can get the coroner down here and forensics. I'm scared to move or touch anything without having more of my team here. I don't want to mess anything up," continued Ron.

"Did you find anything else in there?" asked Hank.

"Yeah, another body.....and if the one is Sally Hanson, I'm pretty sure that the other body is Tim Hanson," said Ron.

"Jesus Christ!" exclaimed Hank.

The two started to head out of the cave. "Listen," Ron said to Hank as they walked toward the entrance, "I didn't want to have to tell you this, but there are 10 children that have all gone missing since 1983, starting with the Hanson's. All of them are tied together by a similar thread, and my guess is that we might find more of them in some of these caves. I figured I might as well let you know at this point as I'm going to need you to show me all of the caves that you know of......because there could be up to 8 more bodies hidden in them."

"Damn," responded Hank, "I'll do anything I can to help."

The coroner arrived a few hours later to recover the bodies along with forensics who documented the crime scene and took as many samples, fingerprints and photos for evidence as they could. Upon a comparison of dental records, it turned out that Ron indeed was right on his hunch, the bodies found were those of Sally and Tim Hanson.

Forensics documented everything but being that it had been so many years, there was no way to discern one set of fingerprints from another or one DNA sample from another for that matter in the cave. Everything was more or less contaminated. All that Ron really had to go on was that two bodies had been found in a cave, and there might be more either in that particular cave or others. He could only hope that further cave searches might lead him to more evidence that would help him solve the case.

Ron got into his car after making plans with Hank as to which cave they might search next. He had a very unfortunate task ahead of him to complete. He would have to tell the Hanson Parents that he had finally found their children, and not alive. Ron didn't even bother to call them, he went straight to the Hanson house, knowing that they would want to know any new information immediately regardless of the time.

It was late in the evening, and he noted as he pulled up that the house was in a state of disrepair. It had been a long time since he had spoken to the family or stopped by the Hanson house, and it looked very different. It used to be a very well maintained home. The grass was always cut, and it always seemed to look like someone had just applied a new coat of paint on the exterior stucco, but this was not the case on that day.

Ron pulled up to see an overgrown lawn. The lawnmower was in the middle of the yard, with cut grass behind it as if someone had started to mow and just given up. The mailbox was overly full, and the paint was fading on the stucco and chipping around the windows.

Ron approached the front door and pressed the doorbell but it didn't ring, so he knocked on the door. He could see through the window in the door that someone was in the living room, but he couldn't really tell who. He knocked again but whoever it was wasn't moving. He knocked again.

"HEY! It's Detective Ron Clark.....I have some information you're going to want to hear," he yelled through the door.

Tom Hanson, father of Sally and Tim, stood up from his lazy boy chair, annoyed that Ron Clark,

who he had not seen in years, was at his door. He stumbled towards the door (a result of alcohol) wearing sweatpants and an undershirt and flung the door open. He looked at Ron in slight disgust.
"What the hell do you want?" Tom slurred in drunken speech….
"I have some information about your case….is your wife home as well?" said Ron.
Tom looked at Ron with a look of rage on his face, "Are you fucking kidding me?!" replied Tom angrily. "In case you haven't heard she's dead you idiot! Slit her wrists upstairs in the bathtub years ago. But you probably didn't know about that did you with all of your other important detective work….." Tom said rolling his eyes.

      Ron had no idea that this had happened. He'd been lost for so many years in the bottom of a bottle that somehow he'd missed that Tom's wife had committed suicide.
"Oh my god Tom, I'm so sorry, I had no idea," said Ron. "I've honestly been drinking a lot over the past few years, and it's no excuse but I've kinda been lost in my own world trying to figure myself out."
Tom laughed out loud "YEAH? Welcome to the club!! My kids disappeared 10 years ago and then 5 years later my wife killed herself….what's your excuse???"
 Ron had no reply. Despite his own personal issues, they paled in comparison to Tom Hanson's current situation. "Okay, fair enough, but I do have information that you're going to want to hear," said Ron.

"Ok fine shithead, c'mon in! You wanna look at the bathroom where my wife died first or just tell me that you finally found my dead kids?!" said Tom.

Ron entered the house, sad to see what had happened to Tom, his life, everything. The house was in shambles…..trash and dirty laundry everywhere. The house reeked of dirty socks, liquor, and body odor. It was absolutely disgusting, even for Ron who wasn't that cleanly himself. Tom was out of shape, and had developed a large beer belly over the years as well.

"Sit down Tom" said Ron.

Tom composed himself and sat in his lazy boy chair, about the only piece of furniture in the room that wasn't covered with garbage or dirty laundry. Ron looked around the room and decided that he was better off standing.

"We found them," said Ron, "in an underground lake in an unknown cave, I'm sorry."

Tom looked up at Ron and smiled. "Perfect! So I'm the only one left in my family? Great……I'm gonna grab a beer, Ill grab you one as well!"

Tom left the room, and Ron just stood there in a state of shock. It took him a moment to process the situation and Tom's response which was unexpected.

Ron suddenly heard a loud bang coming from the kitchen. By the time he realized that the noise that he had heard in the other room was a gunshot Tom was beyond help. Ron ran into the kitchen to find Tom dead on the floor, the victim of a self-inflicted gunshot wound. There was a can of beer on the counter with a note. It read "thanks for trying, I'm with my family now, all of them." Ron had no response. He stood there over the body as it lay on the floor, lifeless, slowly losing blood. Ron picked up the phone and called it into the station. This wasn't how he had been expecting things to go.

The following day

The next day Ron was quite busy, he had to help handle press releases for both finding the Hanson kids as well as Tom's unfortunate suicide. Within a few hours it was all over the news. A cause of death had yet to be determined for the children and there was no concrete proof of how the kid's bodies had actually gotten into the cave, so the press release more or less just let people know that the kids were found, and that upon discovering this Tom Hanson had killed himself.

Tony and Jeff followed the story on the TV news in the breakroom of the warehouse just before starting their shift, knowing that they had found at least one of the bodies. The newscast had stated that the police would be further investigating other caves in the area, so it would be a while before Tony and Jeff would do any further exploring (not that they were planning on doing any exploring after what had happened the day before). Finding the dead body had given them quite a scare, and they weren't about to go exploring in other caves any time soon. They certainly didn't want to find any more bodies, run into cops who were searching for bodies, or even worse run into whoever was behind putting the bodies in the caves in the first place. So for the time being they'd just have to work their jobs, enjoy getting stoned, skateboard, and maybe do some exploring elsewhere.

After sorting out reports to the press, Ron looked through all of the evidence that forensics had found the day before. He went through hundreds of crime scene photos but there wasn't a lot to go on. The caves had been visited multiple times over the years and the crime scene was beyond contaminated. It was impossible to trace anything back to a foot print or a fingerprint as there were too many to count. The coroner's report wasn't helpful either. The bodies had been in the water so long that there was no actual way to determine the cause of death. He wondered if the bodies had ever been seen before but not reported? Surely this couldn't be the first time that someone had gotten into that cave and seen something?

Ron reached out to Hank Grady, in order to set up a time to search some of the other caves that Hank was aware of. They would meet in 2 days' time, planning a full day to search the caves that Hank knew of. Hank did however warn Ron that for all the caves that he knew of, there were also some that he knew existed, but had no idea where they were located. Some caves were along the river bluffs close to the one that they had been in the other day when they found the bodies, but there were some that were long forgotten, caves that only a handful of people knew about, if that. These other caves had no maps or locations on file, and may have never been mapped in the first place. So although Hank could help Ron to some level, he only knew of a third of the caves in the area or so, maybe less than that. For Ron this was okay and it was better than nothing. At least they might be able to find something.

In the days before Ron met up with Hank again, a funeral was held for the two Hanson children, as well as their father. All three were buried next to their mother in Lakewood cemetery in Minneapolis. The family was finally reunited but under tragic circumstances.

Ron attended the funeral, as did several other members of the community. It was an unfortunate ending to an even more unfortunate situation. Ron knew that there were more bodies out there, 8 to be exact, and that the kidnapper and killer of these children was still out there as well.

Chapter 4

A few days later Ron met Hank down by the river close to where they had been a few days before. Hank explained to Ron that there were several caves hidden in this area. The caves were mostly man made and were created for storage, silica mining for making glass and brick, and even mushroom growing and cheese aging. He explained that some of the caves were more dangerous than others, and that some were harder to get into than others.

Hank decided that they should start with the easiest and most accessible cave. Hank led Ron down a long dirt trail that ended near a swamp by the river. At the end of the trail there was a large old slab of concrete which Hank explained was a remnant from a brick company that used to mine for silica in the bluff nearby. He showed Ron what was left of the old brick making kiln that still stood dug into the side of the bluff. Just to the left of the Kiln was a cave entrance, blocked with Iron bars that had been welded over the entrance to keep trespassers out. There was also a door that could be unlocked to open the gate. Hank unlocked the door, opened the gate, and the two entered the cave.

Hank explained to Ron that this cave had been used to mine the sand in order to make bricks, but in recent years had been sealed off. In most cases the city didn't seal off caves with gates but this one was also a cave that was used by bats as a place for hibernation so the cave was sealed in such a manner that people couldn't get in, but bats still could. Kids would dig out around it though and find ways to squeeze in, or bend the bars in order to gain access. Hank said that this was one of the most trafficked caves in the Twin Cities, so chances were that if there were any bodies they'd probably have been reported by now, yet he felt it was still worth a look.

As they entered the cave Ron noticed the usual graffiti everywhere, but he also noticed that the ceilings of this cave were considerably higher than the cave that they had been in the day before. The passages were much wider as well. Upon entering they were in a huge room that was illuminated by the light shining through the gate. There were 3 passages that led off from the main room. And they more or less went straight back, leading to dead ends where in the past the mining had stopped. The third passage had a few paths that led elsewhere but still ended up at dead ends. At one point a bat swooped over Ron's head, startling him but no harm was done.

The two men spent a lot of time looking for something that might be another clue, signs of digging where a body might be, and even wading through the few sections of the cave that were flooded but as Hank had predicted, they came up empty handed. All that they found were old beer cans and trash, an old bicycle that had gotten in there somehow, and the strong smell of residual marijuana from kids who had recently partied in there.

    It was time to move on to the next spot. The next cave that Hank took Ron to was considerably harder to access. They had to go back to Hanks truck and Haul some equipment up the bluff a little way to get to the location. The cave was located down the same trail as the previous cave that they had entered, but the entrance was located about 20 feet up the bluff. The entrance to this one was a straight vertical drop of about 20 feet down and only about 45 inches across. Hank explained to Ron that it was a ventilation shaft for an old cave that was at one time used as a local night club. The shaft would lead them to the cave, but they would need to use the gear that they had grabbed from the truck in order to get in there. Hank had brought the usual gear (hard hats, gas detectors, flashlight and headlamps), but he also had some rope and rappelling equipment.

    He explained to Ron that in order to get into the cave they'd need to rappel down into the hole. He pointed out footholds dug in the sand wall that they could use to climb back out with the assistance of the ropes. Ron had never done any rappelling before so Hank had to take a few minutes to explain to him how it worked. Once Ron had a good understanding Hank tied the rope to a nearby tree. He rigged himself in first to the rappel line and then assisted Ron in doing the same. Hank went first, slowly rappelling himself down the hole into the cave. Ron followed shortly thereafter but less gracefully than Hank.

Upon reaching the bottom Ron put on his gear, and turned on his headlamp and flashlight. As he aimed the light and scanned around the cave he noted how this one was bit different than the previous cave. It was more of a labyrinth, with many small narrow passages going off in multiple directions. He noted some string tied off at the entrance that went into the cave, no doubt used at some point by someone to find their way back to the entrance. He was not worried about getting lost though, as Hank had been in this one before. The ceilings of the cave were only about 15 feet high in some areas, and the side passages connecting areas of the cave only about 5 or 6 feet high and 3 feet or so wide. It made him feel a bit more claustrophobic than the previous 2 caves.

Hank led Ron through the cave, showing him some of the more interesting features. As the cave had been used at one time as a night club there were still a few remnants left behind. There was a part of the main bar still standing, and a few old chairs and tables that were still intact. There were old pipes running along the ceiling used for electrical wiring as well. Much like the other caves that they had visited there was fair share of old beer cans on the floor and broken glass. The walls were covered with graffiti and carvings from visitors past, and there was a faint smell of urine, most likely from either a person or some animal that had at one point lived inside of the cave.

The little side passages winded through the underground space, occasionally opening up into larger spaces that at one time might have been a dining area, bar, or a ballroom floor that probably had live music playing back when the space was still a nightclub. Hank told Ron that it was rumored that some of the famous Chicago Gangsters had used this place as a hideout back in the day, but there was never really any truth behind it or proof, just the stuff of urban legends.

The passages seemed to go on endlessly, and more than once Ron found himself in what appeared to be a new passageway that led him back to somewhere that he had already been. When they got to the back of the cave after covering thousands of feet of passages, Ron noticed something that struck him as somewhat peculiar and out of place. There were a bunch of old tables and chairs piled up against the back wall, along with a lot of trash. Ron got the feeling that all of this junk had been deliberately moved there. Maybe it had just been moved to make more space in the rest of the cave? Or maybe it had been moved there to cover something up.

With Hanks assistance, Ron began moving all of the junk away from the back wall to see if there might be something either behind it or underneath it. It was a slow process as there was a lot of stuff to move. After nearly an hour of moving items Ron noticed something behind all of the Junk. There was a small crawlway through the wall to another part of the cave. Hank told Ron that even he didn't know that it was there and that they should definitely investigate it. The opening was only about 2 feet high and a little over a foot wide so Ron had to go in alone. The space was just a bit too big for Hank to fit into, but Ron was thin enough that he could manage it.

    The passage was longer than Ron had expected. He crawled on all fours through the darkness, with only his headlamp to light his way, occasionally calling back to Hank to let him know that he was okay. It was at least 50 feet before he reached a larger space. The narrow crawlway opened up to a small room, no bigger than 10 feet by 10 feet, with a ceiling equally as high. As Ron got into the room he immediately noticed some displaced sand in the corner and started digging with his hands. He also noted as he was digging that there was no graffiti or carvings in this room. No one had been in there for a very long time if at all.

    He continued to dig in the sand until he hit something about a foot or so down. He moved the sand away to reveal a baseball cap brim, and as he dug further, a body. Ron didn't know whose body he had found this time, but he was certain that based on the events of the previous day that he'd stumbled upon another victim. It was clearly the body of a child, and he was more than certain that there would be another body nearby. The children always disappeared in two's, and so far at least they'd been found that way.

    Ron crawled back out of the tunnel and reported his find to Hank. Once again the entire crime scene team came in, did their investigation, and Ron did his due diligence by taking care of the press release and notifying the family once the bodies had been identified. As he predicted another body was eventually found in the same place. So just as he thought, these two bodies were more than likely related to the Hanson case.

Over the next week Ron and Hank continued to explore the caves that Hank was aware of, occasionally finding themselves in a somewhat dangerous situation. At one point a section of a cave collapsed and they had to find another way out. Another time their gas detectors went off and they were forced to leave the area or face certain death from gas poisoning. They were able to find 2 more additional bodies, bringing the body count to a total of 6. If nothing else, Ron was able to bring some closure to the families after finding the bodies. Luckily for Ron, there were no suicides this time around.

Unfortunately, Ron was no closer to solving the case and Hank had taken him to every place that he knew of. Without having more caves to explore Ron was once again hitting a dead end. Hank had told him that there were more caves out there to be found but that he just didn't know where they were. Ron needed to figure out where these caves were. But how?

A few days later

Ron sat at his desk looking over the evidence gathered from all of the bodies that he and Hank had discovered over the past week. There were still 4 kids missing, and he was almost certain that they were hidden within the caves somewhere. Unfortunately, he had no way of finding them. He had even had the tech. guys at the station look up anything that they might find on computers about the local caves (Ron wasn't exactly computer savvy), but nothing turned up about old caves or their locations. Ron and Hank had looked through all of the old utility maps but again there was nothing there. In the early 90's there wasn't much of an internet to speak of so finding what one was looking for on the internet was not as simple as a google search either (not to mention the slow speed of dial up internet through phone lines back in the day).

    At least Ron had some sort of lead at this point though. He knew that whoever was doing this had a pattern. They kidnapped kids in twos, and thus far each pair of children had been related to each other in the fact that they were victims of the same person, or at least that is what Ron believed. These pairs of children thus far had also been found together. Ron also knew that whoever was behind this was disposing of the bodies in caves. He had yet to determine a cause of death however. Every single body that had been found was too far decomposed to determine this.

    He did know that no children had died from gunshot wounds or physical trauma though, the coroner's report had revealed no physical trauma based on the examination of the bodies, and there were no bullets or casings found by forensics. If only they could figure out the cause of death, Ron might have a better idea. The bodies were also found fully clothed in each case.

    Ron knew that the two in the lake could have been drowned there, but the others were found buried. Perhaps each child had been suffocated to death in some manner? Two drowned and the others buried alive? Ron speculated that the killer must be deriving some sort of satisfaction or pleasure from doing this, and since the bodies were all found to follow a pattern of being hidden in caves, the cause of death would most likely follow some sort of pattern as well. But there was something missing. A piece to the puzzle that he hadn't quite figured out yet. Sure, hiding the bodies in caves was a good way to keep them hidden but they could have easily been buried somewhere else. Why caves specifically? Why would someone go to all that trouble to get the bodies into the caves, or get the kids in there and then murder them? It seemed like a lot of work and there had to be some purpose behind it.

    The bodies that had been discovered so far had been there a long time, and Ron knew that based on the coroner's report that they were the first 6 of the 10 kids to have disappeared given the age of the bodies and their states of decomposition. If he could find the other 4 he might have a body intact enough to determine the cause of death which might help him better understand what was going on.

    It had been a few years since he had received a letter, and he could only hope that he could get to the bottom of this before receiving another one.

Then again, maybe he'd get lucky and wouldn't ever receive another one. Of course then he'd never be able to catch the maniac behind all of this.

He sat at his desk for hours, making notes, reviewing the evidence again and again, looking for something that he hadn't seen before. It was around 4PM in the afternoon, and as he looked through the evidence once again Officer Wallace (the same Officer Wallace who had picked up Tony and Jeff a few weeks earlier) approached his desk.
"How's it going Ron?" asked Wallace.
"As good as it can I guess, I finally have something to go off of with this child murder case but I just can't seem to find enough to figure out what to do next," Ron replied. "I've located 6 of the bodies in caves along the river bluffs but I have nowhere left to look. We've searched every cave that the city is aware of, but there's got to be more out there. I just don't know where to look," said Ron.
 "Well," said Wallace, "maybe you need to find a local expert?"
"Like who?" replied Ron.
"I know of these two kids, just out of high school. They're a couple of local stoners, but they do a lot of exploring around the city. These two know the caves pretty well, heck I've caught them multiple times climbing around the bluffs looking for those caves. They might have some insight into where some of these lesser known caves might be?" said Wallace.
 Ron thought for a moment, he didn't have any other bright ideas at the time and figured that these kids might actually be able to help.
"You know their names?" asked Ron.

"Tony Jankowski and Jeff Larson," said Wallace.
Ron wrote the names down in his notes. "Thanks Wallace, that just might work."
Wallace nodded and added "just so you know Ron these guys don't like cops much, and try to avoid us as much as possible so you might need to call them into the station in order to get them to cooperate."
"Good to know," Ron replied.

Chapter 5

    Tony awoke on a Saturday morning in July. It was already hot and humid in his bedroom from the summer heat outside. His family was too cheap to invest in air conditioning for the house but he was used to it by this point in life. Tony still lived with his parents. He figured that he could stay with them and save up money until he could afford a car and a halfway decent apartment. They were pretty cool about it since he had just graduated and was working a full time job, even if it was a crappy job. His parents basically told him that they'd give him a year to get his shit together. If at that point he wasn't at least enrolled in college or a trade school for something he'd have to move out and support himself. He still had plenty of time to figure that out.
    Tony took a cold shower that morning, not freezing cold but cool enough to wash off some of the heat that filled the house and made him feel all sweaty and sticky. Today would have been a great day to explore a cave he thought. Even in the summer the caves stayed cooler than the air outside, usually around 50 degrees or so giving the effect of

natural air conditioning. Sometimes he and Jeff would go find a cave that they already knew about just to cool off a bit on hot summer days like this day was.

After his shower Tony went downstairs and chatted with his parents a bit, had some breakfast, and then retired to his bedroom to kick back on his day off and play some video games until he heard from Jeff. He entered his room, careful to lock the door behind him and tucked some dirty shirts under the gap between the door and the floor. He reached under his bed, where he kept his supply of weed carefully hidden from his parents inside of a shoe box, and grabbed the shoe box. There was a small stack of Penthouse magazines located next to it as well. The box contained a simple marijuana pipe, a lighter, some Zig Zag rolling papers and a small amount of marijuana capped inside of a film canister (a small tightly sealed plastic can with an airtight lid, generally used for keeping undeveloped 35mm camera film from being exposed, but also useful for keeping the smell of weed at bay). He pulled out a small amount of weed and loaded it into the pipe, went over to his open bedroom window which contained a large window fan aimed to blow air out of the room, turned on the fan, and proceeded to get himself high.

After taking a few hits off of the pipe he made sure that the weed had burned out by covering his thumb over the top of the pipe to deprive any burning embers of oxygen (a trick that he had learned from Jeff after Jeff got busted by his folks in 9th grade by leaving a pipe lit by accident, causing the smell to permeate through Jeff's house after he had left, and eventually leading Jeff's parents to find his weed), and carefully tucked everything back away under his bed. He then lit a stick of incense that he kept on his dresser just to make sure that the smell would be covered, and then sat down on his bed. He turned on the TV and his Super Nintendo, and loaded up Legend of Zelda: A Link to The Past.

He had been stuck on the same dungeon level for weeks on the game. The ice palace dungeon. The Ice palace dungeon was particularly hard to navigate as the character slid around on the screen and was hard to control. Tony wasn't getting anywhere with it and his frustration with it drove him crazy at times.

He played for around half an hour or so, and was startled when his mom suddenly knocked on the door.

"TONY?" she called through the door.

"Yeah Mom?" he responded.

"Get out here," she said in a stern and commanding tone.

"Just a sec. I'm literally almost through this dungeon on Zelda!" he called out.

"Right NOW!" she yelled.

Tony's stomach churned. She only talked to him like that when he was in serious trouble. Did she smell the weed? She couldn't have. He'd been smoking weed in his room for years in the same manner as that day and had never been caught. So what was it?

"Oh shit, what did I do?" he quietly mumbled to himself." Okay be right there!" he called back.

He reluctantly set down his game controller, kicked the dirty shirts to the side of the doorway and opened the door, not really wanting to know what was waiting for him on the other side.

He stepped into the hallway to see his mother looking very upset. Tony's mother was a short, petite woman with black curly hair. But that didn't stop her from being intimidating when she was upset.

"What's up?" he asked innocently, knowing that he had probably done something wrong but couldn't for the life of him figure out what.

"I just got off the phone with the damned cops! Guess who they wanna see down at the station?" she said angrily.

"ME???" Tony responded in disbelief.

Why would the cops want to see him? The last run in they'd had with Officer Wallace had ended without any consequence. Could it have something to do with the anonymous tip about the bodies? If so how would the cops even know that Jeff and Tony had found the bodies? They called from a payphone? What could this be about? Did his dealer get busted and name him or something? His mind raced.

"Yeah, YOU!" his mom replied. "What did you do?" she asked.

Tony couldn't think of anything besides the tip off about the bodies so responded with "nothing as far as I know."

"Well, get your shoes on, we're going down to the station," said his mother.

"Well, so much for a nice relaxing Saturday," Tony thought to himself.

He got his shoes on and hopped in the car with his mother. She proceeded to yell at him the entire way to the station, ranting on about his good for nothing escapades with Jeff and how he needed to figure out what to do with his life. After a few minutes he wasn't even listening anymore, he was more worried about why the cops wanted to see him.

When Tony and his mother arrived at the station they found Jeff and his mother sitting on a bench in the waiting area. "So they got Jeff too," Tony thought to himself. "This has gotta be about that phone call, no way it could be about anything else," he thought. He suddenly regretted smoking weed that morning as it was really starting to kick in and his paranoia was going through the roof.

"Sit there," said Tony's mom and pointed to a chair that was as far away from Jeff and his mother as possible.

She approached the front desk and said,

"Hi, I'm Sarah Jankowski. You guys called in my son about something? You wanna tell me what this is all about?"

"Hold on a sec," said the officer behind the desk, he picked up the phone and made a call. "Yeah, they're both here now," said the officer. "Please have a seat Ms. Jankowski. Someone will be out shortly." Sarah did as she was asked and took a seat next to Tony.

A few moments later officer Wallace came out. He saw both Jeff and Tony in the waiting area with terrified looks on their faces. They both took one look at him and turned white.
"Well hello boys!", said Wallace in his usual condescending tone. "Why don't ya come on back!", Wallace said waving them to a doorway that led into the back of the station.
"Now wait a minute," said Sarah, "My son isn't going back there until you tell me what this is about. Tony may be 18 but I'm still his mother."
Officer Wallace smiled, "Ma'am, there's nothing to worry about. We just want to offer them a job, just some temporary work!"
Jeff looked over at Tony and mouthed out "What the fuck?" silently. Their mothers looked at each other equally confused.
Tony and Jeff were led back to the desk of Ron Clark. Their mothers were asked to wait in the lobby due to something related to confidentiality and the delicate manner in which a certain case was being dealt with. They were assured that their sons weren't in any trouble and that they merely had an employment proposition to make to the boys.
"Have a seat boys," said officer Wallace. Tony and Jeff sat down in two chairs that had been placed in front of Ron's desk. Ron looked at the two boys. They were sort of like twins he thought. Both with long shoulder length hair and dressed in a similar manner. Tony was wearing a Jane's addiction T-shirt, and Jeff was wearing a Pearl Jam t-shirt. Both boys had on ripped up jeans.
Ron looked up at Wallace and said "these two?"

Wallace nodded. "Yep. This is them," said Wallace.
"Okay, thanks," said Ron, somewhat apprehensively. Wallace nodded and walked away leaving Ron to chat with the two boys, who looked frightened and confused.
"So," said Ron, "I heard that you two do a lot of local exploring and know a lot about the caves hidden around the city. Maybe even caves that no one else knows about? Is that true?"
"That all depends on why you wanna know," said Jeff suspiciously.
"Well boys," said Ron, "I'm detective Ron Clark, and I've spent a good part of my career obsessing over a particular case that involves both the kidnappings and deaths of several children. Until recently, the case had gone cold with no leads. But a few weeks back I got an anonymous tip about a child's body being found in an abandoned cave. Upon searching that cave I found not one but two bodies. You probably heard about it on the news. Since then, with the help of the fire department, I was able to investigate and search several other caves in the area and managed to locate 4 more bodies of missing children. I believe these six children are all related to the same case. I also have reason to believe that there are 4 more bodies hidden in caves around the area. The only problem is, I've been in every cave that the city knows about and still can't find these other bodies, bodies which might help me solve this case. I need help finding other caves in the city so that I can search them and I think you two might be able to help. The police department is willing to compensate you for your help. But this

would be a full time deal and I'd need you to be 100% dedicated to this for a while. I don't know how long it will take. Might be a few weeks or even months. Basically what I'd need you to do is show me where these unknown caves are and help me to search them for evidence, so what do you think?" Tony and Jeff looked at each other and nodded with excitement.

"So let me get this straight," said Tony, "you're actually giving us permission to legally enter the caves and are going to pay us for it?"

"Yeah," said Ron, "more or less. I just have to be with you when you do it. In addition, I've been given a budget for equipment. Anything you need. Rope, headlamps, rappelling equipment, hard hats, ladders, all that stuff."

The boys looked at each other and smiled with excitement. This was too good to be true! They were going to get paid to do what they loved and get gear upgrades to boot at no cost to them? They could hardly believe it. Not to mention it would get them away from their boring jobs at the warehouse for a while.

"Hell yeah," said Jeff, "we're in. But you gotta call our employer and explain the situation so that we don't lose our jobs while we're doing this, and you gotta explain this to our parents or they're gonna have our asses!"

"I think that can be arranged," said Ron, "I just need you guys to sign some forms and fill out some paperwork. But before we do that I need to know how many caves you actually know of? Because if

you only know about the ones that I've already been in then we're just wasting each other's time."
Tony thought for a moment. "At least 20, maybe more," said Tony, "but we haven't been in all of them, and some of them we have an idea where they are but not an exact location…..so we might have to search in areas for some of them…..but yeah I'd say at least 20."

"Well, that's at least 14 more than I know about," said Ron, "so that should keep us busy for a while."

The boys sat with Ron for an hour or so, filling out the typical employment forms, W-2's and such. They also had to sign a confidentiality agreement that required them to keep silent about the case to anyone but Ron. In addition, there was a waiver that stated that the police were not liable for injury or death and that the boys were doing this at their own risk. When all was said and done it turned out that the boys would be earning more than they did at the warehouse! They were overjoyed and not even thinking about the dangers that could await them taking on this task. Ron was just happy that they were willing to help. Without Tony and Jeff, he would have been stuck again. Now he at least had a chance of finding something that might lead him closer to the killer. If they could find more clues in the other caves Ron thought that he might be able to finally figure out what was happening, and how to stop it from happening again.

As far as Tony and Jeff were concerned, the first order of business was to get proper gear. They had some basic stuff but if they were going to explore every inch of the caves they would need a

lot more than they had. They gave Ron a huge list of items. They figured that they might as well get as much out of the deal as they could.
The list included the following:

New hiking boots
Hundreds of feet of rope
Portable gas detectors
Rappelling gear
Backpacks
The highest powered flashlights and headlamps that money could buy
Reusable water bottles
Pocket knives
Hard Hats
Respirators
Shovels
Ladders
Several rolls of string
Portable blow torch
Compass
Batteries

    They weren't sure if they were going to use it all, but Tony and Jeff figured that it was better to be safe than sorry. Once they'd completed the list they left the station with their respective mothers. Ron had explained the situation to both mothers without giving away too much but enough to satisfy their curiosity. He explained to the parents that due to the confidential nature of the case that he couldn't tell them much but that their sons would be helping in solving a crime and get paid for their time. This seemed to be enough.

The plan going forward would be that Ron would get the items on Sunday afternoon from the list and they would start searching on Monday morning. He would also contact the warehouse where the boys worked and explain the situation so that they could keep their jobs after all was said and done (even if their jobs were crappy).

Jeff could hardly sleep on Sunday night. He couldn't believe that the following day he would be out exploring caves all day, getting paid for it, and wouldn't have to go work in the damned warehouse again for a while. Although he had some desire to help Ron solve the case, he also hoped that it would take some time because there were a lot of caves that he and Tony had not yet fully explored, (and some that they had not explored at all) and this would be a great opportunity to check them out. In addition to this the more time he spent away from the warehouse the better. He started thinking of where they should go first. The first place that came to mind was a cave that was located on private property. It was along the same bluff as the cave that he and Tony had been in when they found the body, but the property was fenced in and owned by a construction company, being used as a storage yard. Tony and Jeff had staked out the place a few times only to find that there were motion sensors and cameras on the property, and that the cave entrance was covered by a heavy metal door that had a very big lock on it. It was at ground level so it wasn't too hard to get into if one could get past the door. Tony and Jeff had never risked that cave due to the fact that they thought for sure they'd get caught and be charged with trespassing as well as breaking and entering if they attempted it. Jeff figured that'd be a good place to start if Ron hadn't already been there. Jeff eventually fell asleep, dreaming of the adventures that lay ahead.

The next morning Jeff had breakfast with his mom and stepdad. His real dad had left years ago never to be heard from again, but his stepdad was a pretty good guy and worked well as a father figure for Jeff.

Ron picked the boys up at 8 AM with a pickup truck that had been provided to him by the city to begin their search. The back of the truck was loaded with all of the items on the list that they had given to Ron on the previous Saturday. The boys looked over maps that Ron had acquired from Hank, where Ron showed them the places that he had already been. They were all the most commonly known caves, ones that both boys had been in before multiple times.

"These are seriously the only ones that the city knows about?" asked Tony.

"Yeah, these were the only ones that they were able to show me," replied Ron.

"Dude," said Jeff, "there's a lot more out there. I say we start with the one behind that construction company. We've never been in that one."

"Good idea," said Tony.

Ron agreed and the boys hopped in the truck and directed him where to go.

The three of them pulled up at the construction company about 20 minutes later, walked through the gate, and approached the main building which was basically a trailer with a few offices inside. "Wait here," said Ron and went into the building. The boys waited for him outside. Ron came out a few moments later with the key for the lock on the heavy metal door which opened the cave. He held up the key and waved it Triumphantly. "Oh hell yeah!" said Jeff with excitement. The three went back to the pickup truck and collected the basic gear. Headlamps, flashlights, hard hats, extra batteries, water bottles, gas detectors, and a shovel. If they needed more they could always go back. They loaded anything that they didn't immediately need into their backpacks.

As they headed to the entrance Ron informed them that the yard foreman had told him that the door of the cave had been opened and the lock broken off several times over the years, and that the cameras and motion detectors were broken and more for show than anything. So the foreman didn't have any old camera footage that Ron might be able to review if they found anything in the cave.

They approached the cave and Ron unlocked the door. They pulled back the heavy metal door and went into the unknown. As they walked in they turned on their new and improved headlamps and flashlights. They lit up the inside of the cave as bright as a pair of headlights on a car and the beams stretched much farther than the crappy flashlights that Tony and Jeff had used before. They found themselves in a large room that was held up by a few sandstone pillars that had been dug out from the ceiling. The ceiling was about 15 feet high and the room was circular, about 40 feet across or so. The room was filled with old ladders, buckets, scaffolding pieces, and tools such as rakes and shovels. It was clearly being used by the company for storage.

"How did the city not know about this one?" asked Jeff.

"I dunno," said Ron, "maybe they lost the map over the years or forgot about it. All I know is that Hank didn't know about this one," added Ron.

They carefully looked around the room but didn't find anything significant. Ron figured that if there was anything there like a body it probably would have been discovered considering that the construction workers most likely frequented the space for equipment on a regular basis. Based on the footprints on the floor of the cave it looked like at least this area of the cave was used regularly. After searching the room however, they found a small tunnel entrance that had been walled off with cinder blocks. A corner of it had been chipped away at the bottom. Someone had spray painted a warning above the small opening that said 'don't risk it.' Directly below that someone had also spray painted 'it!' There was just enough room for a person to squeeze through. They decided to investigate this area first.

The three of them squeezed through the narrow gap between the cinder block wall and the wall of the cave. It was only about 10 inches wide so just enough to get through. They had to go through sideways it was so tight. On the other side of the wall they found themselves standing in a tunnel but it had been mostly filled in with sand and debris to the point where to go forward they'd have to climb up the sand hill in front of them where there was a gap of only about two feet high between the debris and the ceiling of the cave.

"It's gonna be a crawl to the end of this one," said Jeff.

The three of them climbed up the sand hill to the top and started crawling forward with Tony in the lead, Ron in the middle, and Jeff in the back. The sand was very soft and not very well packed down so it was challenging to move through it. Due to the tightness of the space and the inconsistency of the debris and sand filled floor they were frequently scraping their backs on the ceiling, causing sand from the ceiling to sprinkle onto their heads.

About 20 feet in Tony stopped, ahead of him the passage narrowed even further with only about a 12-inch gap between the ceiling and the debris/sand pile that they were crawling on. "It's getting pretty tight up ahead, I'm gonna keep going but I'm kinda doubting there's anything up there," said Tony. He continued forward despite the small gap.

At this point Tony was now army crawling into the narrow space ahead of him. As he crawled along he hit his knee on a rock which sent a sharp pain into his leg. His body jerked in reaction to the pain causing him to hit the ceiling of the cave very hard with his back. Before he knew what was happening a section of the cave ceiling collapsed on top of him and he suddenly found himself buried underneath it, unable to breath and unable to move from the weight of everything that had fallen in the collapse. He was still conscious and quickly tried to move backwards but was unable to move. It wouldn't be long before he suffocated to death. He tried to hold his breath but the weight of the sand and rocks that had fallen on top of him didn't allow him to do so. He tried to breathe in only to feel sand and dirt fill his mouth. He began to panic. He wouldn't have long to live if he couldn't get out of this but all he could do was lay there and hope that Ron or Jeff could get him out in time.

  Ron, who was just behind Tony, saw the collapse happen and quickly moved toward the collapsed area in order to try to help Tony. He could barely make out one of Tony's feet sticking out of the debris. Without even thinking he pulled on Tony's foot with all of his strength, gradually getting Tony out of the pile that had fallen on top of him. Tony coughed up sand as he was pulled out of the debris. Tony sat up in the small tunnel and looked at Ron.

"You okay?" asked Ron.

"Water…." Tony grumbled as he continued to cough up sand.

  Ron reached in his pack and quickly handed a water bottle to Tony. Tony took a drink, coughed a bit more, and said "I think I'm okay. Damn that was close. No more going that way I guess." Jeff crawled up to see what had happened. Jeff saw that the tunnel in front of them had completely collapsed and that there was no way to get through it.

"You okay Tony?" Jeff asked.
"Yeah, but no more tight crawls like that for me. If Ron hadn't been able to pull me out of that just now I'd be dead. I couldn't move or breathe once that shit dropped on top of me."
"Which Reminds me, let's get the hell out of this area," said Ron.
The boys agreed and they headed back to the storage area.

While moving through the storage area Jeff came across a tunnel leading up hill. Although the gap at the top of the hill was only 4 feet high or so, he could see that it opened up into a much larger space. Someone had placed one of the old ladders from the storage space on the hill to use as a sort of staircase to get up the hill of loose sand that lay in front of them.
"Hey you guys! Come check this out!" exclaimed Jeff. Ron and Tony walked over to where Jeff was standing and shined their lights up the steep hill of loose sand.
"That looks promising," said Ron, "Let's go."

The three of them headed up the steep hill using the ladder for footholds on the loose sand. The hill went up around 30 feet and through the narrow 4-foot gap. On the other side of this they found themselves inside of a gigantic room with a ceiling that was nearly 50 feet high! The sand hill went up further topping off about 20 feet from the top of the giant dome of a ceiling. "WOW! This is huge!" said Tony in disbelief. "We should climb to the top of the hill and scan around the room to look for gaps that might lead to other areas!" They slowly scrambled

their way to the top of the hill. Without the ladder to use as steps at this point it was a somewhat treacherous climb. The sand was very loose so as they climbed their feet sunk several inches into the sand, it was like climbing a hill of unpacked fresh snow. They more or less had to crawl up to reach the top. Upon reaching the top of the hill they could see that the top of the ceiling was almost perfectly circular and the room itself was easily over 100 feet across. They did a 360-degree scan around the room noticing the way that they had come in by the ladder down below, but down the hill in other directions there were more gaps similar to the one that they had come in through that appeared to lead to other areas of the cave.
"I think we should climb back down and walk around the perimeter of this hill to check out those gaps and see if they lead anywhere," said Ron.

The boys agreed and the three of them slowly went back down the hill, half walking and half sliding. They went one at a time in case the hill decided to landslide on top of one of them. Upon reaching the bottom of the hill there was an awkward and uneven path that led around the perimeter. They came across 2 gaps that led to spaces that were more or less filled in with sand. Not wanting to risk another collapse they avoided them and didn't go in.

They then came to another gap similar to the one that they had come in through that went downhill into another section of the cave and it appeared that it led to an open tunnel. There was no ladder to use as steps this time so they had to slide and crab crawl their way down feet first, again going one at a time in case of a landslide.

When they got to the bottom they found themselves in a large hallway of the cave that went on for quite a distance in both directions. The ceilings were about 15 feet high and the hallway was equally as wide, big enough to drive a truck through. They went to the left first down the hallway which led to what appeared to be another door going into the cave from the outside as they could see light coming through from somewhere. There were no signs of bodies or hidden areas where they might be found however so they went back in the other direction. As they headed down the hall of the cave in the other direction they came across a few ladders that leaned up against the walls but led to nothing. Upon further investigation they started coming across old strings of Christmas lights, and even an old plastic light up pumpkin! They could only figure that either someone was using this as a place to store their holiday décor or that there had been some parties there back in the day. They even came across what appeared to be a small stage that had been built towards the back of the hallway where it appeared to be leading to a dead end. They wondered what it could have been used for and then went past it to see what lay ahead.

Behind the stage it looked as if there was nothing left but some junk piled up to a dead end, but Tony noticed that there was a small hole about two feet wide and two feet high that led into what looked like another hallway. They crawled through the hole and found another passageway but it had

been filled in a lot with sand so was only about 4 feet high from floor to ceiling. The three crawled through the passage for fifty feet or so until they reached another small tunnel leading to the left. When they crawled through it they found themselves in a small room that was about 20 feet across with ceilings of maybe 12 feet. There was an old Honda motorcycle parked there against the wall, and what appeared to be old bench seats from either a van or maybe a minivan. Jeff looked at the motorcycle and then back through the tiny hole that they had just come through. He seemed perplexed.
"How the fuck did this thing get in here?" Jeff asked, referring to the motorcycle and comparing it to the tiny hole that they had just come through.
"The cave wasn't always filled in like this dumbass. That's a '78 Honda CB 750. I'm sure someone stole it back in the day, took it for a joy ride, and then dumped it in here long before the construction company owned the land around it and back when you could probably just walk right in here," said Tony.
"Oh, yeah DUH!" said Jeff. Ron laughed at his response.
    They found a few more tunnels after looping back to the big room with the sand hill, and they even found a very sketchy staircase carved into the sandstone that led upward for nearly 100 feet, but didn't find any bodies or evidence of foul play, so after giving the cave a full look over they decided that it was time to move on to another cave.
    Ron locked the door as they left and returned the key, thanking the foreman for letting

them have a look. They went back to the truck and hopped in. As they drove to the next location that Tony and Jeff had suggested, the boys finally fessed up to Ron that it was them that had made the phone call about the first body. Ron said that he had already figured as much but didn't blame them for not telling him sooner.

They explored two more caves that day, ones that the boys had been in before but Ron hadn't. But once again they had no luck finding anything that would help the case. By this time, they were tired, hot, and dirty. One of the caves had been flooded and they had had to wade through 2 feet of water for most of the search, the other one was full of muddy clay that stuck to them like glue, so at this point they decided to call it a day and continue the search the following morning. Ron dropped the boys off at their homes and told him that he'd be back to get them at the same time the following day.

Tony didn't sleep well that night. He dreamt that he was back in the cave where they had found the body of Sally Hanson. He kept seeing her body in the water, and then the cave would collapse in on him. In the dream when the cave collapsed, unlike what had actually happened, no one was there to rescue him, and he would wake up right before he suffocated to death. He'd eventually fall back asleep, but the dream would keep coming back to him over and over. He eventually gave up, smoked some weed and played Zelda on his Nintendo until the weed finally put him to sleep.

Chapter 6

    Ron picked the boys up in the morning just like the day before and off they went on another adventure. Tony told Ron that today they'd be going to a different area, closer to Minneapolis. There was a very big cave system that they'd heard about along the river that had multiple levels and went on for miles under the bluffs. The only problem was that they didn't exactly know where it was, just the general area, so they'd have to climb around on the bluffs to find it. Tony was certain that they could find it this time unlike previous attempts that Tony and Jeff had made in the area. In the past they'd had to be stealthy about looking for the cave as sometimes cops went by in boats looking for cave explorers as well as homeless people that lived along the bluffs. They didn't need to be sneaky about it and worry about being seen by anyone this time since they were with Ron, so it would be easier for them to search for the cave. Tony and Jeff had been in the area twice before and never found the cave, so they also knew at this point where not to look.

They parked in a residential area near the bluffs along Johnson Road. Johnson road ran above the bluffs so in order to find this one they'd have to scale down a very steep bluff with a lot of loose dirt, sand, and rocks to get to the cave which was supposedly near the base of the bluff. This section of the Bluffs was particularly dangerous because unlike the parkway area, at the base of the bluff was a cliff that dropped 30 feet to the river below with a depth of only about 3 feet of water at the river's edge. So if one was to slip and start sliding down the bluff, even if they could control the slide, there was always a chance of falling over the edge, crashing into the water, and smashing onto the rocky riverbed with nothing to really break ones fall. This would almost certainly lead to injury or possibly death. Luckily they had enough rope that they could tie off at the top and rappel their way down.

Jeff insisted that they bring the ladder in order to reach the tunnels that might be above them within the walls of the cave once inside. He also thought that they might need it to climb down to certain areas as the cave supposedly had more than one level. Tony agreed and despite the weight of it all determined that they should bring all of the equipment so as not to have to climb back up the bluff to get anything else. They loaded everything into their packs that they could, and carried everything else.

They tied the rope to a fence at the top of the bluff which they then used to lower down the ladder. The ladder would get stuck from time to time so they repelled down behind it, moving it when it got lodged between trees or stuck on a rock. It was a slow process to get down there, and the drop down was nearly 300 feet at an angle of at least 65 or 70 degrees. Very steep. It was a hot day and all three of them were sweating buckets as they worked their way down the bluff to the edge of the cliff that fell off into the river.

When they got to the bottom they could see a path that went in both directions, at times going uphill and at other times down. It ran right along the edge of the cliff so one slip and you'd be falling 30 feet into the river below. There were sections of the path that had eroded over time as well so in some areas the path was only a few inches wide requiring anyone attempting it to put one foot directly in front of the other like they were walking on a balance beam in order to get to the next area.

They decided to head west first, as it looked a bit less dangerous and they could see sandstone exposed in the side of the bluff which could possibly lead them to the cave that they were looking for. Jeff led the exploration this time, with Ron in the middle and Tony bringing up the rear. Carrying the ladder and all of the gear made walking the path all the more difficult. There were some places where the path had eroded away completely and Jeff would have to jump across and have Ron pass the ladder across to him before jumping himself. At one point the gap was so wide that they had to lay the ladder across it and crawl over the ladder in order to get to the other side.

After hiking along this path for a while they came to an inset of sandstone along the bluff where

there was an opening about 5 feet high and two feet wide in the bluff. Jeff, overcome with excitement immediately entered before the other two could catch up but was quite surprised at what he found. He walked into the cave to find a very small room, more like a root cellar than a cave. It was only about 15 feet deep with maybe 8 foot ceilings.
He flipped on his headlamp only to find a strange man sitting there who said "Hey man what's the big idea! You trying to blind me!"

As Jeff's eyes adjusted to light he realized that he was staring at some old homeless man who had a paper bag in his hand and what appeared to be paint around his mouth. The man was quite dirty and his long gray hair was matted and had clearly not been washed for some time. He had a long gray beard and was wearing an old trench coat. Jeff noticed that there were several empty cans of spray paint on the floor of the little cave but no graffiti to speak of. He realized that he had stumbled upon the dwelling of some crazy paint sniffer who had probably lived there for years based on all of the junk that was in the little room.

"Oh, ah, hey man. My fault. I didn't know anyone was in here," Jeff said startled and apologetically.
"It's cool man! You just scared me! You wanna huff some of this with me?" said the old man offering his brown bag of paint fumes to Jeff.
"Ah, maybe some other time?" said Jeff awkwardly. At this point Tony and Ron walked in to see the strange scene that Jeff had stumbled upon.
"Oh, hey guys!" said the old man as Ron and Tony entered, "welcome to my pad! I ain't got much but

you can huff some paint with me if you like?" Ron raised an eyebrow and flashed his badge at the strange old man.

"I think we're good on that buddy," said Ron.

"Oh….yeah……I get it. Sorry," said the old man, suddenly concerned that he might be in trouble.

"You might be able to help us with one thing though," said Ron. "We're looking for a big cave system that is supposedly along this path somewhere. Any idea where it is?" The man thought for a moment,

"Oh yeah!" said the old man, "The big one? I never go in there cuz of all the bats but it's back the way you came, maybe a mile or so. Right down the same path. It's really big though. I've seen people go in and never come out I swear!" the old man exclaimed.

"Thanks," said Ron.

"No problem!" said the old man.

They walked out in the same order that they had come in with Jeff following last.

"Uh….sorry to intrude on ya dude…..enjoy your paint!" Jeff said as he left.

The old man smiled and laughed revealing mouthful of rotted and missing teeth. Jeff cringed at the sight of the man's rotten mouth for a moment and then followed Ron and Tony back out onto the bluff.

They had no choice but to go back over the section of the path that they had already covered. They eventually came back to where they had started, passing the rope that they had used to get down there in the first place and headed in the other direction over the more treacherous section of the path.

The path was much hillier in the other direction, forcing them to follow up and over sections of hills that had loose sand and shale rock. It was tough for one to get good footing and all of them slipped a few times as they walked along the river at the base of the bluff. More than once they came across an eroded gap and had to once again lay the ladder across the gap and crawl across it in order to get to the other side.

They eventually came down to a spot low enough that the overhanging cliff was no longer an issues and they were more or less right along the shore of the river. Jeff noticed an area of sandstone in the bluff about 20 feet ahead and about 15 feet up the bluff. It looked promising. When they reached it he climbed up to the sandstone wall and at first he saw nothing, but then noticed a small entrance, no bigger than 15 inches high and about 2 feet wide. "I think I found something!" he yelled to Ron and Tony.

The two came up to where he was standing and agreed that this could be the cave that they had been looking for. Jeff shined his light into the hole and could see that the narrow entrance went back quite a way. They were going to have to crawl their way in, and getting the ladder in there was going to be a challenge.

They were able to get in and maneuver the ladder, but they had to get through about 25 feet of crawling in order to do so. It took them about 20 minutes just to get in with the ladder but they eventually made it. Upon entering the cave, they found themselves at the start of a long man made hallway in the cave, it went back so far that they couldn't see the end of it. To the left there was a small tunnel, and to the right another long hallway. It appeared that there were several other hallways running perpendicular from the two that they could see in front of them, and they could see that some of these tunnels headed upwards while others headed down. It could definitely be a multi-level cave system. They decided to head down the small tunnel to the left first. It was very tight and they left the ladder behind. The little tunnel was just high enough to walk through in a crouched positon and the floor was wet from some sort of flooding. The tunnel went on for about 15 feet, opening up into a large storm drain which ran down the bluff next to the cave. The drain was walled off to both the left and the right, so it was just a dead end.

      They then headed back down the tunnel to the main cave passageway. When they again reached the large hallway, they started to walk down through it. To the right there were a few shorter tunnels but they mostly led to dead ends. To the left however there were longer tunnels that led to another large tunnel that connected and ran parallel to the main hallway tunnel. The cave was basically set up like a ladder, 2 long tunnels that ran parallel to each other with 'rung' tunnels going in between the two. As usual the walls were covered with graffiti and carvings. The ceilings ranged anywhere from 15 feet to 30 feet high and the width of the hallways anywhere from 12 feet to 20 feet wide. As they got further back into the cave they noticed that the ceilings and hallways were much larger.

They wandered through the ladder cave system, zigzagging back and forth through the connecting hallways and back to the main ones in the front and back of the cave. There were also some little tunnels that they found along the way. One led downward to another section of the cave that opened up into a second set of tunnels that were dug underneath the ones that they had come in. They didn't find anything in these lower tunnels but the size of the cave was quite impressive.

They eventually found their way to the far backside of the cave, the bottom of the ladder so to speak, or the top depending on how you want to look at it. This was where the ladder system ended and it seemed like the cave just sort of wound around aimlessly with tunnels and passages turning off in multiple directions. At the back of the cave the ceilings were much higher as well, nearly 40 feet high in some areas. Some of the larger rooms in these spaces had pillars in the middle dug out of the sandstone holding up the roof of the cave. There were a few small tunnels heading upward, but they ended after 50 feet or so in small rooms. Tony surmised that these might have been air shafts that had eroded or maybe even old entrances that had been sealed off over the years. There was no way to know for sure.

At the far back of one of the tunnels they found a narrow passageway that led back a long way. It was only about 4 feet high. When they got to the end of it, it opened into a huge space, a giant room with ceilings of nearly 40 or 50 feet in height. The room itself was at least 300 feet across. The only problem was that the tunnel that they came in through was about 20 feet above the floor of this space. They had to go back and grab the ladder that they had left at the entrance in order to get down there.

When they got back with the ladder they were able to lower it down and safely climb down to the floor of this large room. There was little to no graffiti in this space so it had clearly not been visited as often as other areas in the cave.

They searched around the room in hopes of finding one or more of the other missing bodies but again their search efforts were in vain. There was nothing there. No bodies, no sign of disturbed earth that would lead one to believe that someone had been buried there. Nothing. So once again their efforts had been in vain. It took them over an hour to get back out of the cave and back up the bluff to the pickup truck. At this point they were all exhausted and decided to once again call it a day. They made plans for the following day for new caves to investigate.

They spent the next several days exploring other caves in the area but were no closer to finding the other bodies or any evidence that might help the case. They were all beginning to feel a bit discouraged and began to wonder if they'd ever find the other four bodies that were still missing or anything that might help them solve the case. It wasn't until about a week later that they finally stumbled upon something that would help further the investigation.

Chapter 7

Tony awoke on a Tuesday morning. He noted that his body felt quite sore from all of the exploring that he had done recently and his muscles ached. They had been in 8 different caves so far and found nothing. He was hoping that today would be different. Today they were heading to a giant cave known as the gangster cave as it had been rumored that back in the day the cave had been used as a hideout for gangsters and criminals. Tony and Jeff had been in this cave before but it was so large that there were even sections that they hadn't seen before. Parts of this cave were filled in with rubble, the remnants of an old bridge that was torn down and used to backfill the cave in order to discourage explorers in the 80's. Of course the local explores just found ways to dig it out or climb around it to get back into the more open areas of the cave. The gangster cave was so large that one could easily get lost, and people had died in there in the 80's due to carbon monoxide poisoning so there was a gas risk as well.

Unlike some of the other caves that they had been inside of, the gangster cave was actually a series of caves that were connected by one tunnel or another and had passages that wound in every conceivable direction, with countless little crawl tunnels going off even further. The last time Tony and Jeff had been in the gangster cave they had gotten lost and found themselves going in circles for over an hour before finding their way back to the entrance. They would definitely need the roll of string to leave as a marker in order to find their way back.

    The cave was located up a short hill in the river bluffs behind an office building. It had been filled in by the city more than once but more entrances had been dug out over the years. Tony and Jeff knew of at least one way to get in.

    Ron picked up the boys with all of their gear in the morning as usual and they headed to the cave. Unlike the last one it was a short trail up a hill to the entrance which was easy enough to get into. Once inside they were in a small room that went back about 20 feet and was filled with ruble from the bridge. It looked like a dead end but if one went forward 10 feet or so there was a small hole about 3 feet by 2 feet that opened up into the actual cave on the left side.

    Upon going through the entrance they found themselves in a large high ceilinged room that was about 20 feet wide. There were 2 small openings on one end of the room, and on the other end was what used to be an opening but had been walled off with bricks. Someone had taken a hammer to the wall though and knocked away enough bricks in the middle to create an opening about 3 feet across. They decided to look here first. The bricks appeared to have been knocked away recently.

They walked across the room toward the small hole in the brick, making sure that their gas detectors were turned on. Tony went first, Ron in the middle, and Jeff in the back. Tony flashed his light into the room to make sure that there wasn't a drop on the other side and found that the hole led to another room similar to the one that they had just been in, with a few small tunnels leading off in other directions. The floor of the room was full if old pieces of timber and bridge rubble, but was big enough to stand up inside of. The floor on the other side of the wall was more or less the same height as the room that they were all currently inside of, so there was no drop into the other room. The ladder wouldn't be needed.

Tony climbed into the room, instructing Ron and Jeff to wait while he took a look around. He walked around the room, shining his light into the tunnels that connected to it, but found that all of them were collapsed or filled with rubble. "Dead end," Tony said and climbed back through the hole in the brick.

They then headed toward the small openings on the other end of the room. Tony and Jeff at least knew these two tunnels; they would lead to some very large hallways in the cave that would have several tunnels leading away from them. If they stayed in the main tunnel it would eventually loop back around to the same room that they were currently inside of. It was at this point that Jeff suggested that they tie off the string and use it as a trail marker. The last thing he wanted was to get lost in this cave again. He knew that the last time that they had been in there it seemed like every main tunnel led off to several other small tunnels that continued to lead on to other large tunnels and just continued on like that forever. It was like a maze and several of the rooms looked very similar to each other as well as the passages. It was easy to think that one was in a certain main tunnel and then realize later that it was a different tunnel or not the same small tunnel that one had gone through before. It was a very confusing cave system to say the least.

  They went through the small tunnel to the left first, which was really more of an entrance to another area as it only went about a foot before opening up into a much larger section of the cave. They left the ladder and some of the bulkier gear behind and would come back for things if needed. On the other side of the tunnel they found themselves in a very large passageway. It seemed to go on forever in two directions. The ceiling was at least 30 feet high in the passageway and the walls rose up to meet at a point at the top, giving the passageway a feeling like one was inside of a giant underground castle.

"Wow, this one is pretty big!" said Ron.

"You just wait, this is only the first passage….it goes on forever," said Jeff.

"I was in one like this when Hank was showing me around, with the pointed ceilings," said Ron, "but it was a lot easier to navigate than this one," he added. "Yeah dude, it's an old mine. The mines always have the high pointed ceilings for some reason," said Tony.

Ron couldn't believe the size and length of the passage. This was clearly the largest cave that he had been in so far and he couldn't believe that there was even more to it. They would definitely be in here for a while. If there were other passages of this size and magnitude with other tunnels leading off from them they could be there for hours. They might even need to make more than one trip?

They headed down the tunnel in one direction, slowly unraveling the string as they went to leave a trail marker. The passage was so wide that they could all walk next to each other with plenty of space to spare. Based on the size of the cave, Ron was certain that there could be a lot of places to hide a body and they would have to conduct a very thorough search. He could see how Tony and Jeff had gotten lost in this place before. Ron reached into his backpack and grabbed out the compass. He noted that they were travelling in a southwesterly direction. They walked down the tunnel slowly, scanning the area for other side tunnels or anything that might lead them to another body. They came across one side tunnel that they made note of to visit again later but decided to follow the main passage to the end first. After about 500 feet they came to a dead end. They turned around and headed back down the tunnel in the other direction,

double checking to see if they'd missed anything besides the one side tunnel. The passage started slowly going uphill and up ahead appeared to level off. Ron could see something ahead reflecting light off of his flashlight. It appeared to be made of metal.
 "What's that up ahead?" asked Ron.
"You'll see," Tony said with a smile.
	They walked further down to the passage until Ron could see what was reflecting the light and was quite surprised to see a full sized trampoline, about 15 feet across, in the middle of the passageway. As they approached it Jeff ran up to it, climbed onto it and began jumping up and down on it.
"What the hell?" Ron said.
"Some kids brought it in here back in the day when the cave entrances were bigger!" Jeff said as he jumped on the trampoline.
"C'mon Ron! I know we're doing serious business here but you have to jump on it at least once! It's a tradition in this cave!" yelled Jeff as he hopped off of the trampoline.
	Ron obliged the request and made a few jumps on the trampoline followed by Tony. Ron noticed that there was a small passage about 20 feet above the trampoline that they could most likely get to with the ladder. So that made 2 different side tunnels off of this passage so far, not counting the one that they had entered through.
	They continued down the long passage which at times went downhill and then back uphill. They eventually came to another brick wall which at some point had blocked the passage, but like the

wall that they had seen earlier someone had knocked it out with a hammer so that there was a small entrance through it, leading further into the cave. A graffiti artist had spray painted a monsters face with teeth around the hole in the brick so that it appeared as if one was going into the monster's mouth while going through the little entrance.

When they got to the other side of the wall the passage went on for another 50 feet or so and had 2 side tunnels on either side, one of which led them back to where they had started and where they had left the gear, and the other one led to another gigantic passage just like the one that they were currently inside of. Before going into this new passage, they decided to go back and check the other two small tunnels that they had already found back by the trampoline. They grabbed the ladder before going.

They walked with the ladder all the way back to the other end of the passage to where the first side tunnel they had found was located, leaving the ladder by the trampoline as they went so that they could use it on the way back.

As they got to the other end of the passage once again they looked into the small tunnel that went off in another direction. It was half covered by bricks but wide enough to fit through. On the other side of the bricks was a drop of about 3 feet into a narrow passageway that was about 5 feet high and 3 feet wide. They squeezed through the entrance and dropped onto the floor. The tunnel went straight ahead but as they passed through it they noted several doorways that went into little rooms on either side, framed in by wood. It appeared that these may have been storage areas for equipment at some point. There was no sign of a body in any of these rooms though so they kept going.

Eventually the narrow tunnel opened up into a larger space, much like the first large passage that they had encountered with the trampoline, but this passage was more backfilled with bridge ruble and dirt than the previous one. It also wasn't nearly as long. A tunnel continued on the other side which led them to more similar backfilled spaces. Eventually they came to a dead end and headed back until they got back to the trampoline.

They set up the ladder to reach the opening above the trampoline some 15 or 20 feet up. Jeff climbed up and entered the narrow tunnel which was also a very steep climb. There were old bricks lining one side of it like some sort of shaft. It may have been an air shaft or used for transporting something down into the cave at some point but he couldn't be sure. He eventually reached the top about 50 feet up or so where he could see a little light coming in from the outside. Maybe it was used as an entrance at some point? All Jeff knew was that it was another dead end. He climbed back down and shook his head. "Nothing," said Jeff.

They decided to go back through the wall with the monsters face and try the other passage in that area. After passing through the wall once again with the creepy monster's mouth they came upon the small tunnel, which was only about 3 feet tall. "We haven't been in here before," said Jeff.

It led into a large open space with a very high ceiling. To the right a path went uphill to a 3-foot-high ledge that then rose to another passage. To the left it went downhill and then wrapped around to the right. They went to the right only to find that after climbing the 3-foot ledge that the path went downhill, wrapped around a section of rock, and then looped back to the passage they had seen on the left. They went back down and this time followed the opposite rock wall to the right which led them to one of the most impressive spaces Tony or Jeff had ever seen in a cave.

It was a very large room shaped somewhat like an egg. In one spot in the room there was a little hill that led to a throne that someone had carved into a piece of sandstone. The ceilings were quite high, and the room itself was easily the size of a basketball court if not larger.

They didn't find any sign of foul play, but Ron was beginning to understand the urban explorer fascination with cave exploration. He was pretty impressed by what Tony and Jeff were showing him. The three walked back after searching the giant room and were about to head back when they came across a small passageway to the left. The passage led uphill for about 5 feet and the floor was so narrow at the base that you had to put one foot directly in front of the other in order to get through it, but it was wider at the top. There were pieces of bent rebar metal jutting out through the walls as well. The look and feel of the passage was different than the other parts of the cave and it was more than likely that this was a passage that led to a completely different cave system. They decided to go in, being careful not to catch themselves on the jagged metal sticking out from the walls as they went.

They found themselves in a low ceilinged room which was mostly backfilled. There were however passages to the left and right which appeared to open up. One of the passages had a giant mushroom spray painted over it. They decided to try that one first. They walked over the backfill and down through the mushroom entrance.

They entered a low ceilinged room that was full of pillars about every 12 feet or so that the cave had been dug around. Along the walls there were several little spaces dug out of the sandstone to form chairs of sorts. There was broken glass everywhere as well as empty beer cans and other trash. This was clearly a party space. The room had a faint smell of marijuana as well as an even more overpowering smell of urine.

"This room reeks like piss," said Ron.

"And weed," said Jeff giggling.

They wandered around the room which appeared to have had a different purpose than the rest of the cave. It didn't appear to be a mine and seemed more like an event space.

"Did we just find the old tavern?" said Tony as they looked around the room.

"Old tavern?" asked Ron.

"Yeah," said Tony. "You already went into the one with that other guy that was a night club back in the day before you started searching with us. We were told by some other guys who explore that there was an old tavern connected to this cave. This is just the first time that we found it. If we go back the other way I think, there's an old bowling alley or what's left of one?" he added.

"Interesting," replied Ron.

Although the tavern room was interesting there were no signs of what they were looking for and the smell of stale urine got to be a bit much for all three of them so they went back through the mushroom entrance, up and over the backfill, and then down through the other side of the room. This led them to a long hallway. As they walked through the hallway they came across some old tables and benches that looked like they might have been part of the taverns furniture from back in the day. As they travelled further they found what was left of the bowling alley that Tony had mentioned. There was no longer an actual bowling alley, just some planks of plywood and a set of plastic bowling pins with a ball, the type that little kids would play with. But beyond that was another side entrance that looked promising.

It was a small tunnel that led through for quite a distance. It looked to only be about 3 feet high and equally wide. It would have to be a lengthy crawl to get through it but it could lead to something so it was decided unanimously that they would attempt it.

Jeff led the way, with Ron in the middle and Tony in back. As Jeff looked ahead he could see no end in sight so he knew that it was going to be a long crawl. The tunnel curved around to the left so it was hard to see where it ended. At one point Jeff thought that they had reached a dead end when they literally ran into a brick wall blocking the passage. However, much like other walls encountered in the cave they found a section that had been knocked away and were able to squeeze through it and keep going. It was a good thing that they had used the string as a marker as they had gone a long way in and at this point Jeff wasn't 100% sure if they would have been able to find their way back out without the help of the trail marker left by the string.

After crawling through the tiny tunnel for what seemed like forever, it finally opened up into a small room. Before entering Jeff scanned his light around and noticed that about 4 feet into the room there appeared to be an opening in the floor, or perhaps a drop? He had to crawl closer to take a look.

When he got to the edge he looked down. It was a giant hole about 10 feet across! The hole itself was circular and lined with bricks all the way around. The drop to the bottom was at least 30 feet, maybe more. Too far for the ladder to reach, and Jeff couldn't imagine going back to where the gear was and hauling that back and into the tunnel. He did however think that rappelling down the hole could work. He could see at the bottom that there was a small hole knocked out of the brick as well. It might lead to something so it was probably worth a look. Ron and Tony found their way to where Jeff was and looked down the hole.

"We're going to need the ropes and rappelling gear, the ladder won't reach down that far," said Ron.

"I was thinking the same thing," said Jeff.

Tony volunteered to go back and get it. He could use the string trail to find his way back to the gear as well as back to their current location. The others agreed and waited while Tony went to get it.

Tony followed along the string that they had unrolled as they had travelled through the cave, eventually finding his way back to the gear. He gathered up all of the ropes and rappelling gear and began heading back, following the same trail left by the string.

As he wandered back he found that being alone in the cave was much creepier than having an exploring companion. The silence in the cave was in a way terrifying, and any noises that could be heard made the hairs on the back of Tony's neck stand on end. He kept telling himself that anything that he heard was just the wind (even though he knew that there was little to no wind deep inside of a cave) or the ground shifting. At one point he heard what sounded like the voices of children in the distance, but he told himself that it was just his mind playing tricks on him. As he travelled back to meet the others he thought more than once that he saw something move, and had a strange feeling as though someone or something was watching him, but again he explained it away as his own paranoia. He moved as quickly as he could back to where Jeff and Ron were located, and was somewhat relieved when he got there.

"Man," Tony said, "I'm not going anywhere in a cave alone again. That was beyond creepy dude."

Jeff Laughed.

"We're gonna have to find a place to tie off the rope before we rappel down. I'll show you guys how to do it if you need me to," said Ron.

"No need my good man!" said Jeff, "This ain't our first rodeo."

"Fair enough," replied Ron.

There was no place in the room itself to tie off the rope but Jeff remembered some pieces of thick rebar metal sticking out of the brick wall that they had squeezed through that could work. Jeff crawled back in the tunnel until he reached the wall. He tied the rope off, giving it a few hard tugs to make sure that it was secure, and then headed back to the hole where Tony and Ron awaited him.

They all took a few moments to get rigged up with rappelling gear and then looked back down the deep hole that was lined with bricks.

"I wonder what this was used for?" said Ron.

"I dunno man, I've never seen anything like this in any of the caves we've been in. It almost looks like part of a building but we're so far underground I can't imagine anyone building something like this in here. I guess it could be part of an old basement from a building that used to exist above but no way to tell….maybe there were stairs at some point and it was storage for the tavern and bowling alley? Who knows," said Tony.

"I'll go first," said Ron, "I weigh more than you guys so I'll be a good test for the rope and tie off. Plus, I don't want you two risking your necks if you don't need to. "

Ron lowered himself into the hole, slowly rappelling down in the way that Hank had showed him only a few weeks ago. The rope held thankfully as he didn't know what he would have done had he fallen. He noticed as he climbed down that in some spots the brick had fallen out of place, allowing him to use these gaps in the strange circular hole as foot holds to stop for a moment. It reminded Ron of an old well, the kind that people would lower a bucket into in order to get water back in the day, but it was much larger in circumference so he surmised that it couldn't be a well.

As he got closer to the bottom he started to notice a strange and somewhat putrid smell. He looked at his gas detector which was attached to his belt and the readings appeared to be good, so whatever he was smelling, it wasn't dangerous gas. He started to hope that what he was smelling was decaying bodies. Normally this would not be something that one would hope for, but for Ron a smell like that could mean a lead in the case.

When he got to the bottom and finally landed on the sandy floor he took a look up. He figured that it was around a 35-foot drop. It was going to be tough to climb back out. "Only one of you should come down here," he yelled up to the boys, "just in case we can't get back out. The other one should stay up top to either help us out or go for help if needed. You guys can decide who goes down and who stays up."
Tony and Jeff looked at each other.
 "Rock paper scissors?" said Jeff.
"Works for me," said Tony, who secretly didn't want to be the one left alone after being creeped out

earlier. They did 3 rounds, and Tony won the best 2 out of 3.

"You won Tony. You choose. Staying here or going down?" said Jeff.

"Going down," said Tony.

"Good luck," said Jeff, and patted Tony on the shoulder.

Tony smiled and slowly started lowering himself into the hole to meet Ron. It didn't take him long to get to the bottom. As he disconnected from the rappel line he asked Ron "What is that hellish smell? That's downright nasty!"

Ron replied "my guess is there's something dead inside that hole there."

Ron pointed his light toward a small hole at the bottom of the well like space that they were standing inside of that was at most 20 inches across and maybe 2 feet high.

"We're going to have to look in there," said Ron, "there might be dead bodies in there so I understand if you want me to go first."

"Umm, no offense Ron, but can you even fit through that hole? " asked Tony.

Ron laughed and said "yeah I'm pretty sure I can squeeze through there."

Ron got down and peered through the tiny hole. He could see that it opened up to a room or maybe a tunnel on the other side that curved off to the right. In order to actually see the inside of the room however he would need to go in. Ron got down on his stomach and began sliding through the hole. The putrid smell became much stronger as he wiggled his way in.

Ron found himself in a small space with a rounded ceiling, only about 4 feet high and maybe 5 feet wide. Unlike the other parts of the cave there was no graffiti at all. Much like areas where he'd found the other bodies no one had been in here in many years which to Ron was a good sign that he might find something. He followed the room around to the right. It appeared to sort of wrap around the outside wall of the large bricked hole that he had come down in the first place. As he came around the corner he stopped in shock at what he came upon.

The room came to a dead end, and at the far end lay not one but 4 bodies! All of them children. Two of them lay face down as if just thrown in there while the other two, dressed in summer attire, appeared to be huddled together for warmth sitting against the wall in a corner of the space. Ron thought that they may have died of hypothermia in the coldness of the cave, and had huddled together to try to stay warm. This meant that if Ron's assumptions were correct, they had been brought in alive and left there to starve or die of other natural causes. This was his first indication of how all of the other children could have died. Ron couldn't be 100% sure at this point, but he was pretty sure that the kids had been brought in there and then left for dead in the darkness of the cave. This could have been how the other kids died as well. This would explain at least partially why the bodies were all being found in the caves in the first place. But why suddenly 4 bodies instead of two? Up to this point the killer had always left the bodies two at a time. Was the killer getting lazy? Was this a better hiding spot? Ron wasn't sure, but what he did know was that he had more information than before, and he could see that the bodies were fairly well preserved in this location. It was colder down in this hole than other parts of the cave so it was possible that the temperature had played a factor in their preservation, that and the fact that the bodies had been placed down there more recently. Ron began to wonder how this killer had even gotten them down there?

Before doing anything else Ron yelled back to Tony who was waiting on the other side of the hole. "Tony, I found them. All four of them! I'm coming back out," said Ron as he worked his way back to Tony.

Ron and Tony made the challenging climb back out of the hole with the help of Jeff. It wasn't easy to get out. It required a lot of upper body strength to pull one's self out of a hole that deep even with the proper gear, but with some help from Jeff pulling from the top they were able to get out.

They gathered up their gear and worked their way back to the entrance of the cave. Once they got all of the gear back in the truck they headed to the station. Ron reported their find and a crew of officers went in to retrieve the bodies and gather evidence in the cave.

Ron sat at his desk with the two boys across from him.

"Well boys, I guess this is it?" said Ron, "I can't thank you enough. I never would have found the other bodies without your help."

"Do you think you have enough to catch this sicko?" said Jeff.

"It's hard to say at this point," replied Ron, "but I do have more than I did before and that's thanks to the two of you." They shook hands and the boys left the station.

Tony and Jeff stood outside of the station.

"Well," said Tony, "it's been exciting but I guess it's back to the warehouse for us!"

Jeff looked at Tony and rolled his eyes. "Ugh, not good. You got any weed on you?" asked Jeff. Tony smiled and pointed to his backpack and the two headed home.

The evidence from the investigation showed that the 4 children that were found had either died of starvation or hypothermia as Ron had predicted. There were also traces of sedatives in their systems, leading Ron to believe that the children were first drugged and then brought into the caves. The dept. increased patrols around caves in hopes that they might catch the killer going back to visit his victims but all that they ever found were more kids like Tony and Jeff trying to sneak into the caves.

At this point at least Ron knew more than he did before. Whoever was doing this was clearly kidnapping the kids, drugging them, and then leaving them alive deep within the caves to fend for themselves and eventually die. Maybe the killer was monitoring them to make sure that they didn't escape but he couldn't know for sure. It was just a theory at this point. What he didn't know was why and maybe never would. At least at this point he had some sort of a profile on the killer, knew the way in which the kids were dying, and how they were being killed. He just needed to come up with a motive and that might give him an idea of who was behind this.

Chapter 8

1967

Chris Thompson was a 10 years old in 1967. He was pretty scrawny and small for his age, wasn't very athletic, and had fine black hair, parted in the middle. He'd had a pretty rough go at life so far. His parents were poor hippies who didn't take very good care of him. They were young and more interested in using drugs and partying with their friends than dealing with the responsibilities of parenthood. It was pretty normal for there to be random people staying at their home or partying there on any given day or at any given time, even in the middle of the night. Chris had more or less been the result of an accidental pregnancy on his parents' part, and neither his father nor his mother were really fit to be good parents.

Their home was always a mess and reeked like marijuana, cigarette smoke, and stale beer. There was always dirty clothes and garbage on the floor, so much so that there was literally just a path between the mess from one room to another. It was disgusting and no way for a 10-year-old boy to live.

Chris had come to the belief that his parents didn't care about him. They never cooked for him and he primarily lived off of cereal and milk, that is when there was actually cereal and milk in the house. At least he was on free lunch at school and could be guaranteed breakfast and lunch on school days. Chris' parents never got him gifts on his birthday or Christmas, and they didn't seem to care whether he was there or not. Sometimes he would go out to play for hours and they were never concerned if he returned after dark or even noticed if he was gone for that matter.

Chris' mom worked as a waitress at a topless bar and his dad worked at a gas station, when they actually went to work. They lived in a rundown area of Saint Paul in a house that was falling apart at the seams, and rather than try to fix up the house or move to a better part of town, his parents spent all of their money on drugs and booze.

Chris tried to stay positive and be happy despite his living situation, but his life was tough. At school he didn't really have any friends and was often picked on and made fun of for smelling bad and wearing dirty clothes (his parents rarely did laundry). No one really seemed to care for him or worry about him, and he kept to himself most of the time.

Chris didn't even have any real toys to play with other than broken ones that he found in people's trash around the neighborhood. He did like to draw though, and at one point he had found a box full of green pens in a teachers' desk at school which he had stolen. There were around 30 pens in the box and he kept them hidden in his bedroom so that he could draw with them and at least enjoy making sketches when his parents were partying with their friends in other parts of the house.

Chris liked to draw pictures of things that he saw in the neighborhood. Trees, parks, hillsides, and so on. He was actually pretty talented but no one seemed to care. At one point his art teacher even made fun of him for always drawing with a green pen, not knowing that green pens were all that Chris actually had to draw with in the first place.

So this was more or less how Chris went through life; eating when he could, going to school, drawing, and avoiding his crazy parents and their weird hippie friends whenever possible. It was a very sad existence for him and he was often angry at the cards that he had been dealt in life.

In the summer time Chris liked to walk to nearby parks and lakes and draw sketches of what he saw. Sometimes others kids would approach him to see what he was drawing and ask him about it, other times kids would take his drawings and tear them up, laughing at him. He got bullied a lot by kids in the neighborhood and was often beaten up by other kids. When he'd tell his parents about it they'd just tell him to toughen up and deal with it. Chris was not a very strong kid and was an easy target.

Chris only had two friends in the neighborhood, if you could even call them that. Their names were Paul and Troy Boswell. They lived down the street from him. They were a few years older than Chris. Like Chris, they were both poor and were usually wearing hand me down clothes that weren't very clean. Paul was the older of the two. He was very slender and had messy red hair and freckles. Troy was short and a bit on the chubby side, with light brown hair.

Sometimes Paul and Troy would be nice to Chris and play with him, but other times they would pick on him, ditch him somewhere, or get him into trouble. Chris tolerated this because at least they were nice to him some of the time, which was more than he could say for anyone else. Paul and Troy were the only kids in the neighborhood who ever asked Chris to come out and play. The only problem was that Chris never knew which version of them he was going to get on any given day. One day Paul and Troy would just want to just hang out and play, and the next they'd have some sort of scheme in mind and would just end up messing with him, hurting him, or torturing him in some way or another.

Once they had taken his sketch pad and tore it to pieces in front of him while he cried. Another time they had convinced him to climb up on top of a building with them. Chris was scared to climb back down and they just left him there. He was up there for hours before a local cop found him and helped him down. When the cop brought Chris home and explained the situation to his parents as to why Chris had been missing for so long, they didn't seem to care. The fact of the matter was that they hadn't even noticed that Chris was missing.

Another time Paul and Troy climbed into the window well of a nearby school and left Chris there when he couldn't get himself out. He eventually got himself out but by the time he did they were both long gone. They also stole his bicycle and threw it into a nearby pond more than once, forcing Chris to dig around in the murky water to find it.

There were also other times though when they'd all go to the park and play tag for hours without incident, and despite the fact that the Boswell boys both picked on Chris and were often mean to him, they also stood up for him at times. It was sort of like they were allowed to pick on him, but no one else was. Paul and Troy also had a secret fort that they had built in the woods along the river that they used as their clubhouse. Chris was the only one besides them that knew about it and at times he used it as a place to get away from home. Especially if he knew that Paul and Troy wouldn't be there to mess with him.

Paul and Troy came from a broken home as well, so at least Chris had that much in common with them. Paul and Troy's parents were physically abusive to them, which as a result left both boys with a mean streak that was unpredictable, and that was why at times they were nice to Chris and horrible to him at others.

So, even though Paul and Troy were mean to Chris about half the time, the rest of the time they were nice so Chris figured that it was better than nothing. Plus, they'd shown him some pretty cool stuff over the years like cool places he could draw by the river, playboy magazines, and strange abandoned buildings scattered around the neighborhood.

One summer day Paul and Troy were walking up the street and saw Chris sitting on his front stoop with his sketch pad.

Paul yelled up to Chris "Hey Sis!......I mean Chris! What are you drawing?"

"Probably naked ladies from the last playboy we showed him," chimed in Troy, giggling.

"Oh, hi guys! How's it going?" asked Chris.

Paul and Troy approached Chris. "I'm just drawing a cat that I saw in the yard yesterday," said Chris.

The two Boswell boys looked over the drawing and Chris hoped that this would be one of the times that they wouldn't tear up his artwork.

"Why do you always draw with a green pen?" asked Troy.

"It's all I have," said Chris.

"I bet we could lift some pencils from the drugstore," said Paul.

"C'mon! We'll help ya steal some," said Troy.

"I dunno guys, I always get caught doing stuff like that," said Chris.

"Don't be such a pussy! C'mon we'll get you some pencils and then we've got something really cool to show you. It'll be fun!" said Troy.

Chris reluctantly set down his sketch pad and went along with the Boswell boys.

The three of them walked down the street towards the local drug store, Paul and Troy messing with Chris the entire way. They tripped him a few times with their feet and threw fake punches, giving him two hits in the shoulder each time he flinched yelling "Two for flinching!" But when they got to the drug store they were serious about helping him get some pencils.

Troy went and asked the clerk where he could find rubbing alcohol in order to distract her while Paul went into the school supply aisle, grabbed a 10 pack of pencils, and stuck them down his pants. Troy made an excuse for not buying the rubbing alcohol and the boys left. When they got outside of the store Paul pulled the pencils from his pants and handed them to Chris. "Thanks," said Chris. Unfortunately, the clerk saw the hand off and came running out of the store. Paul and Troy ran off and Chris was left standing there with the pencils in hand. He looked up at the clerk and held out the pencils.

"I'm sorry," said Chris, "it was their idea." The clerk was a bit surprised to see that of all the things that could have been stolen it was a pack of pencils. Usually kids stole candy or other sweets.

"Why are you trying to steal pencils?" asked the clerk.

"To draw with. All I have at home is some green pens," said Chris.

The clerk, feeling a bit sorry for Chris said "I tell ya what, you keep em'. But don't let me catch you trying to steal from here again."

"Okay I promise I won't. Thank you," said Chris.

"And stay away from those Boswell boys, they're never up to any good," the clerk added.

"Okay," said Chris.

Chris headed back down the street towards his house. About halfway home Paul and Troy came out from behind some bushes.

"Hey you got the pencils!" said Paul.

"The clerk let me keep them," said Chris.

"How come you guys ditched me again?" asked Chris.

"Hey man we had to run, it's not our fault you just stood there," said Troy. "You got the pencils so who cares?" added Troy.

"C'mon, we've got something cool to show you," said Paul.

Chris reluctantly followed the two boys, pencils in hand. They made sure not to walk past the drugstore again and headed through the neighborhood until they came to the river parkway and began hiking along the dirt path.

"Where are we going?" asked Chris.

"We found a cave!" said Troy.

Chris thought that a cave would be pretty cool to see and could give him some inspiration for drawings as well so he went along.

Paul and Troy led Chris to a path off of the parkway that led into the river bluffs. Before he knew it they were deep in the woods. Back in 1967 there was a lot less built up around the bluffs than there are these days. It was mostly wooded with the exception of some buildings near the marina.

It wasn't long before the boys found the entrance to the cave. Unlike later years the caves entrances were wide open at this time. Some of them were even still in use for things like growing mushrooms, storage, and cheese aging. It was very easy to access them and one could just walk right in as opposed to crouching, crawling, or even sliding into them on ones' stomach.

Chris looked at the entrance as they approached it. It was at least 10 feet high and around 16 feet wide. He immediately took a mental image in order to be able to draw it later. The boys led Chris into the cave. Troy pulled out a flashlight from his pocket and turned it on.

Chris followed the boys as they went deeper and deeper into the cave. Without the flashlight he wouldn't be able to see anything and even with the one that Troy had brought along it wasn't very bright and difficult to see where they were going. They led Chris down several passages, turning left and right to the point where Chris had completely lost his sense of direction. Then, the flashlight went dead. Or so Chris though.
"Paul the batteries died!" yelled Troy in the darkness.
"Oh no, we better go get help!" said Paul.
"Chris you wait here with Troy. I'll try and find my way out to get help."
"Okay," said Chris, a little scared at this point as he stood frozen in total darkness.

Chris couldn't see an inch in front of his face, even after his eyes had adjusted to the darkness. If he had been able to see, he wouldn't have liked what he saw. In the darkness, Paul pulled on Troy's shirt sleeve to follow him, and the two of them worked their way backwards in the dark until they were far enough away from Chris to turn on the flashlight, which was in fact not actually dead. Chris

had no idea that this had happened, nor did he even know that Troy was no longer with him. He thought that he was waiting in the dark with Troy for Paul to return. Troy turned on the light, the two of them giggled, and they left Chris behind in the cave to fend for himself.
As they exited the cave Paul said "he'll find his way out right?"
"He'll be fine. It'll help him build some character," said Troy. Paul laughed and the two headed home.

      Deep down in the cave Chris called out to Troy who didn't respond. He then called out for Paul. It didn't take him long to realize that the two boys had played a trick on him again. He had no idea where he was and no idea how to find his way out. A sense of dread came over him and he felt as if the darkness of the cave was collapsing in on him. He began to cry, not knowing what else to do. How could they do this to him? He suddenly wished that he had just stayed in his yard and worked on his cat drawing. He had no idea which direction the cave entrance was at this point and was terrified that he wouldn't be able to find his way out. Maybe they were just messing with him and would come right back? They'd done that to him before. Then again there had also been times where they'd left him in a tight spot never to return, like the time he was stuck on the roof or the time that he had to climb his way out of the window well. He could feel the packet of pencils, still in his hand, and clutched it to his chest, as if it were some sort of comfort for him that at least he got some pencils to draw with instead of green pens.

He sat there, crying for what seemed like an eternity, occasionally calling out for Paul and Troy, but no one responded. He had been in the middle of the cave hallway when the flashlight went dead and couldn't even tell where the walls were at this point.

After waiting in the darkness for what seemed like forever, Chris determined that it was more than likely that the Boswell boys had left him for dead, and he would have to find his own way out. He started by crying out for help as loud as he could, but he eventually lost his voice, and no one was responding anyway. No one would be able to hear him this deep inside of a cave.

His next move was to try to find his way out. He began moving slowly forward until he could feel the wall with his hands. He began to follow along the wall, moving very slowly, hoping that if he stayed along the wall in the darkness he might eventually be able to find his way to the entrance. He did this for what seemed like hours but had no better idea where he was than when he had started. For all he knew he might be going deeper into the cave as opposed to out of it. He could even be going in circles, covering the same area over and over again. It was useless. He sat down on the floor of the cave. Hungry, thirsty, and tired.

Any ordinary kid would have expected their parents to start to worry at some point and come looking for them. But Chris knew that his parents were too busy partying with their friends to come looking for him or even care. They never even checked on him in his bedroom so why would they come looking for him? On top of that it was summer so even the school wouldn't be noticing his absence. He was completely helpless unless Paul and Troy decided to come back for him.

He began to cry again and laid down on the cave floor. Eventually, overcome with exhaustion, he fell asleep. He awoke several hours later, feeling weak and tired. The air in the cave was cold which gave him quite a chill. He was now very hungry, very thirsty, and couldn't see anything which seemed to lead him to become more and more disoriented. He almost felt weightless and his equilibrium was all out of whack from the darkness.

He decided to start feeling his way along the walls again. Maybe if he paid close attention he could notice cracks in the wall or bumps that he could then use to determine if the wall he was touching was a new one or one he had been to before. He also remembered that some of the passages that Paul and Troy had led him through were little tunnels so he also used his foot along the lower part of the cave wall in order to feel for these openings.

He decided to go to the left, or what he though was the left. The problem was, in complete darkness, he couldn't tell what side of the cave tunnel wall he was on so it was impossible to tell if he was going back the way he had already come, going forward, or just walking back and forth. It was starting to drive him mad.

He followed one section of wall that had a unique bump on it that he could feel, followed by an area where the walls were wet. This eventually led him to a dead end and he started feeling his way back, past the wet spot and the bump, and moving on from there. He found his way to a gap in the wall and went through it, hoping that this would lead him toward the entrance but he really had no idea. At this point, without knowing how long he had slept for, and having no sense of time, he figured he'd probably been in the cave for at least 12 hours, maybe even a day. He felt along the walls again until he was exhausted and once again laid himself down on the cave floor. When he awoke he realized that he had lost his sense of direction again, meaning he couldn't tell in the darkness which direction to go. He was getting hungrier and thirstier by the hour, and feeling weaker with every hour that passed. He felt like he wouldn't survive much longer at this rate.

  He tried to start where he left off the last time he had been awake but he couldn't be 100% sure. He once again felt his way along the wall, and found another little gap to crawl through. As he felt along the wall however he felt a familiar bump followed by a section of the wall that was wet. He realized that he had just walked back to where he had started the day before which was extremely defeating. However, now he was completely familiar with this area and it didn't take him nearly as long to find his way back to where he had fallen asleep the second time. He was slowly finding his way out, or so he hoped.

  He started working his way back from where he had slept the night before and was overjoyed when he saw something up ahead. He couldn't tell if it was his eyes playing tricks on him in the dark or not but he thought he saw light up ahead. He followed along the wall until he reached it. Sure enough there was light coming in but it was from a hole in the ceiling. Just an old air shaft. There was enough light to see that water had dripped down the hole and onto the floor of the cave, creating a small pool in the sand. He immediately cupped his hands and took a drink. It didn't taste particularly good, and Chris knew that it might make him sick, but at this point he had no choice if he wanted to stay alive. He drank a few gulps full before moving on. Now he had another spot where he would know he had been before if he got lost again, and if the water didn't make him sick, he could come back to it and drink more if needed. He yelled for help a few times up the hole in the ceiling, hoping that someone might hear him, but there was no response. Chris decided to move on, making note of the area and the passages that led to and from the small pool of water that was just barely illuminated by daylight. It was the first time that he had been able to see in days and it took his eyes some time to adjust. At least now he knew that going back past this area led to nothing, and he could only hope that the other direction would lead him out. He figured that the daylight wouldn't last forever and he would need to remember this if he came back past the area after dark. Of course there would be no real way to tell unless he stumbled upon the pool of water once the sun went down.

    Chris moved forward past the lighted area as the cave slowly went black again. He felt his way along the wall and came to another small gap that led to a different area of the cave. It was a short tunnel, one that he though he remembered coming through with Paul and Troy, but he couldn't be sure. He was very tired at this point, and hungry. The water that he had discovered had at least given him a little strength to move on but not much. He was beginning to think that he might die in the cave unless someone found him. He figured that between sleeping and moving around in the cave it had been at least a full day, maybe two. But at this point it was hard to tell without having any way to tell time and no daylight to determine how much time had passed.

    Once Chris got through the gap in the wall he headed left. From memory he knew that heading to the right would bring him back towards the way that he had already come through. He felt his way along in the darkness, again making mental notes of places where the walls were wet or there were any unique bumps along the wall of the cave to help him tell if he was back tracking at all.

    He felt his way along the walls for what seemed like hours, hoping to find something to help him get out. Then, almost out of nowhere, he heard a sound that gave him hope. It sounded like a car passing along a wet road way off in the distance. Chris determined that what he had heard might have been coming from the road near the cave. He might actually be close to the entrance! He became very excited and followed where the sound had come from, hoping that this might be the way out.

    He came to another gap in the wall, and had to decide to keep going along the wall that he was currently touching or he might risk a new passage that could lead him back into the cave instead of toward the exit. He decided to wait to see if he heard the sound again. He waited for a very long time, but then the sound came again. This time louder than before. He could tell at this point that it was not coming from the gap but from further down the tunnel that he was currently inside of. He skipped over the gap and kept following the wall down the passage.

After 10 minutes or so he heard the sound again. This time even louder. He continued to move towards the sound. Although he couldn't see any light ahead of him Chris figured that he was probably on the right path.

He didn't hear the sound again but as he felt along the wall he began to see a glowing light ahead of him. He followed the tunnel toward the light and found himself outside shortly thereafter. It was dark outside and the moon was nearly full. The glow that he had seen was that of the moon and some street lights from the road near the cave. Had it not been for the moon and the sound of passing cars he could have missed the entrance completely. The ground was wet and it had recently rained.
He found his way to the road, having no idea what time it was but knowing that it must have been late as he didn't see any more cars on the road. He was exhausted, but decided to try to walk his way home rather than wait around for someone to come by and help him.

When he arrived at home he looked at the clock in the kitchen. It was 1:00 in the morning. The way Chris figured it, he had been in the cave for nearly two full days. He was starving so he looked in the fridge. There was no milk of course. He went to the cupboard and was able to find some cereal though. He poured himself a glass of water, grabbed the box of cereal, and headed towards his room upstairs. He passed his parents in the living room on the way who were passed out on the couch. His dad opened his eyes as Chris passed him and said "go back to bed," and passed out again. They hadn't even noticed that he was gone.

Chris went to his room and gorged himself on cereal and water until he fell asleep. Despite being very dirty from crawling around in the cave he was too exhausted to shower. As he slowly fell asleep, he realized that at some point he had dropped the packet of pencils in the cave. That was the only reason that he had gone with Paul and Troy in the first place! After this experience he had determined that he needed to stay away from them going forward or he would certainly end up dead.

He fell asleep due to exhaustion but his sleep was filled with nightmares of being trapped in the cave. He didn't know it yet, but the experience had traumatized Chris and he'd never be the same again.

Chris awoke the next morning and took a shower. After getting dressed he sat down on his bed, grabbed his sketch pad and a green pen, and began drawing everything from the cave that he could remember seeing. He wanted to remember the places that he had been and what he had experienced despite the fact that it had traumatized him.

After some time, he went downstairs to tell his parents what had happened. He wanted Paul and Troy to get into trouble for what they had done. In the past he had been afraid to report them for fear of retaliation, but this time he didn't care. His parents were sitting on the couch in front of the TV getting high as usual. He tried to tell them what had happened but they weren't really listening. His dad nodded along with his story about being trapped in the cave but was more interested in watching the TV. When he finished telling them what had happened they just told him to go out and play. They hadn't even listened, didn't care, or were too high to notice what he was telling them. He told them that he had nearly died and they just blew it off. This infuriated Chris. How could they not care? Why didn't anyone care? He swore that one day he'd make them care no matter what it took.

Chris went down to the local police station to see what they might do to help, but the police didn't really believe Chris. They thought that he was exaggerating his story and made no effort to even talk with Paul or Troy's parents.

Chris went home in tears. No one cared about him, not even the police. No one cared that he had nearly died in that cave. It was as if it hadn't even happened as far as everyone else was concerned and it made Chris furious. Chris headed back from the police station, being careful to avoid Paul and Troy's house. They were the last people that he wanted to see at this point. He went to his room and drew some more images from the cave, and eventually began to cry. Why did things have to be so difficult for him? It wasn't fair. He felt that he deserved better.

He eventually laid down on his bed and cried himself to sleep. That night he dreamt of darkness as far as he could see. It enveloped him and he was being thrown around by it in a dark, shapeless void. He felt around for walls or floors but there was nothing. He was in an endless black hole for which there was no escape. He woke up several times, his body covered in sweat, but each time he fell back to sleep the same dream came back to haunt him.

Each night the same dreams came back to haunt him, being trapped in the cave or just trapped in darkness. He felt overwhelmed with dread most of the time, and could only shake the feeling temporarily if he was able to distract himself by drawing or doing something else. But the feeling always returned, no matter what he did.

A few weeks later he walked past Paul and Troy's house. Their furniture was in the front yard of the duplex that they had lived in. A neighbor was out mowing their lawn and Chris asked about the furniture. The neighbor told him that the family had been evicted, and would not be living there anymore. "Well, at least they're gone," he thought. "Now they can torture some kid in another neighborhood."

Despite his efforts, Chris was never able to shake the fear and trauma caused by his experience in the caves. The dreams were less frequent, but they were still there as was the fear. He decided that the only way to overcome this would be to confront it. He would have to go back to the caves and explore on his own until he had overcome his fear.

Chris scrounged up any money that he could, finding coins in the couch at home, and doing odd jobs around the neighborhood. He used the money that he had saved to purchase a flashlight, and a few sets of batteries.

He started by exploring the cave where he had been abandoned by Paul and Troy. Finding his way back to the places that he had already been when he was trapped, and exploring new areas in the cave as well. This did actually help to some extent as his fear of caves and darkness started to subside. He discovered several other caves in the area as well as some in other parts of the city, but he never forgot what had happened to him, and he never got over the fact that no one seemed to care. The anger and fear continued to grow inside of him as time went on. Someday he'd make everyone pay for what Paul and Troy had done to him. Someday everyone would pay for ignoring him and neglecting him. Someday......

1993

Chris sat in the living room of his house, watching TV. He was now 36 years old. He had a wife, and a stepson. He worked for the city at the parks and rec. dept. where he helped with park maintenance, clearing brush, repairing playground jungle gyms, clearing snow in the winter time, and other odd jobs that required custodial or maintenance work. He'd been doing it since he had graduated from high school. The job had odd hours so depending on the day he might be working at any time, even in the middle of the night. Sometimes he had to work long hours overnight as well. This allowed him the freedom to come and go as he pleased, with no concerns from his wife or stepson.

Chris still held on to the fear and anger that he had experienced when he was young, and was never able to shake it completely. In fact, it had festered and grown inside him over the years. He still had nightmares about being trapped in caves and darkness, and there was only one thing that would temporarily bring him peace. It wasn't a good way to deal with it, but it did work.

Chris got tired of watching TV and walked out to the back yard and into the garage. The garage had an attic space above that he kept locked at all times. This was his personal space and he had made it clear to both his wife and stepson that this was the case. He was a good husband to his wife and a good father figure for his stepson so neither of them seemed to mind that he had this space set aside for himself despite the fact that it was a little strange. He told his wife that this was where he went when he needed to be by himself or relax. He had made it clear that he needed this space to his wife long before he married her, and she to her son.

The attic space was semi-finished, with a chair, coffee table, TV, VCR, and stereo set up inside. Chris kept a box of VHS tapes and cassette tapes in a wooden box in the attic along with some drawings, which was also always locked (just in case his stepson got curious and found a way in). The contents of this box were Chris' personal secret, and he only opened the box when he was sure that no one would be around. On this particular day everyone was gone and wouldn't be home for hours, so it was a perfect day for Chris to enjoy what was inside of his secret wooden box.

    Chris headed up into the attic, being careful to lock the door behind him, and opened up the wooden box that sat in a corner of the room. Inside of the box there were a few cassette tapes, and a few VHS tapes, each one labeled by a year between 1983 and closer to the present.

    Chris pulled out the first of the cassette tapes and popped it into the stereo. It was labeled "Hanson's, 1983." He put the tape in and pressed play. The tape played back a recording. It was a recording that Chris had made years ago with a cheap Panasonic tape recorder and had listened to many times. He closed his eyes and tried to visualize what was happening, at the time that he had made the recording he didn't have a video camera yet, so he could only listen to the audio and use his imagination.

    The recording itself was of Sally and Tim Hanson. It was the two of them waking up in the darkness of a cave, screaming for help, and eventually drowning in the cave lake where their bodies had been discovered by Tony and Jeff so many years later. Chris had kidnapped and killed them both, (or one could say that Chris had kidnapped them, drugged them, and then left them in a cave to die much like he nearly did all those years ago), and he had made recordings of the events from inside of the cave, unbeknownst to the two children.

Over the past 10 years Chris had been responsible for the deaths of 10 children. He knew that what he was doing was wrong, but it brought him relief to see others endure the pain that he had once suffered. He loved how it affected the community, and it felt good to transfer some of the pain and fear that he still experienced onto others. Chris made recordings of all of the children that he had watched die over the years, starting with audio tapes and later moving to video when it came to be more affordable and less clunky to carry around. Chris never actually murdered any of the children directly, instead he watched sadistically from afar using night vision goggles as they slowly died or met their demise in other ways within the cave.

Some starved to death, some fell down a hole in the caves, and some even died of carbon monoxide poisoning. In Sally and Tim Hanson's case, Tim had wandered into the underground lake by accident and panicked in the darkness. Sally had tried to rescue him, and both of them drowned. Chris was currently listening to Tim screaming and Sally trying to help him as they both slowly drowned.

Chris would kidnap children from time to time, drag them into the caves, and watch them die. When he did this, a sense of relief would wash over him for a long period of time and the anger and fear from his past would subside, at least temporarily. The recordings and video helped to sustain this state of relief for him over time. Eventually however, he'd feel the need to do it again in order to regain that sense of calm that only came when he kidnapped two more children and watched them die. He would sometimes imagine that the children were actually Paul and Troy from the old neighborhood. If only he'd been smart enough back then to lure them into a cave and do the same to them that they had to him. If they hadn't moved away it would have certainly happened. If someone had only helped him back in those days maybe he wouldn't even be doing this now?

After the children would die, Chris would hide the bodies within the caves for the most part, unless he felt that they were already somewhere that they wouldn't be found. He was doing a pretty good job of it as well until recently when a local detective, Ron Clark, had started to find the bodies (the same Ron Clark that he had enjoyed taunting with the letters over the past ten years). This didn't bother him though. He figured that by the time that the bodies were found that there wouldn't be enough evidence to catch him.

He had determined however, that when it came time to do it again that he'd have to find somewhere new. The caves along the river bluffs were now patrolled regularly and he didn't want to risk getting caught. The cops didn't know it was him yet, but they knew what he was doing as well as where, and if he wasn't careful he'd be caught.

He knew of at least one cave that was far off from the others that he had found as a kid, right in the middle of the city. If he needed to act again that's where he would go. The cave was located in the middle of a local nature park and as far as he could tell, no one knew where it was beside him. Whenever he visited that particular cave there was never any new graffiti or garbage. Not even any new footprints. As far as Chris knew he was the only one that knew about it.

    The cassette's audio came to an end, with the sounds of splashing and screaming that eventually ended in the sound of water hitting the shore of the underground lake. The sound of the water eventually turned to silence as the waters calmed, being that Tim and Sally were no longer moving, and Chris turned off the tape and put it back in the box. Despite the poor audio quality this was still Chris' favorite recording. He even liked it more than the videos. Perhaps it was because it was his first kidnapping, or maybe it was because the children drowned unexpectedly?

    The sense of relief that he often got from listening to his recordings was starting to wane however. He knew that it wouldn't be long before he would need to act again. He could tell with each passing day that the fear and anger was starting to intensify again. He was losing sleep, and the nightmares were returning more frequently. He reached into the wooden box and placed the cassette inside.

    There were also several sketches inside the box that he had made over the years of the children trying to find their way out of the caves. The sketches were done in green pen. As he had gotten older Chris had access to other types of writing utensils but for some reason he had become accustomed to using green pens as a kid and just stuck with it. He pulled out a few of the drawings and looked through them. His personal favorite was one of two children huddled together for warmth in the darkness against a cave wall. They eventually died of starvation or maybe hypothermia. Sometimes he went back to the cave to visit their bodies which were still in the same position as the day that they had died, just like the drawing that he was currently looking at. Chris even used the same space to hide two more bodies at one point. As far as Chris knew from the news reports these bodies had yet to be found. He had a video of the two children in this particular drawing and decided to give it a watch.

1987

In 1987, Chris had kidnapped two children, Dante and Elijah Cartwright. He had kidnapped them in the same fashion as the others, coaxing them into his car, and then giving them candy that was drugged with sleeping pills. At the time of the kidnapping Dante was 10 years old and Elijah was 11. Both boys came from an African American family. Chris took them to a cave that he knew of in the area just like the others before them. He did this late at night when there was little to no traffic along the river parkway, and used his work vehicle so that if anyone did come across him and ask what he was doing, he could explain it away with work excuses. He had already planned to drop them into a hole that went down 35 feet or so in the cave, the same hole where Ron Clark later found them dead. Chris had already done his research and knew the cave well. He knew that there would be no way out for them once he lowered them into the hole. He had already been down there and knew that there was no way out. Chris spent an hour or so dragging their bodies to the back of the cave. He used a rope to lower them into the hole, and then set up his camera to film them, using a night vision setting. He turned on the camera, waited for them to wake up, and began recording.

The video

Dante awoke to find himself surrounded by complete darkness. He couldn't remember exactly what had happened. He and his brother Elijah had been playing in the park, and someone they knew from the neighborhood had offered them a ride home. After that he had forgotten what had happened. Was he in his bedroom? Where was he? He felt around and realized that he was in a very cold space, and that the floor underneath him was either sand or dirt. He was definitely not in his bedroom. Nor was he in his bed. He was very disoriented by the darkness and called out to his older brother Elijah.
"Elijah? Elijah are you there?" he said with a tone of panic in his voice.
"I'm here," said Elijah, who had awakened only a few minutes before him.
"Elijah where are we?" asked Dante, hoping that his brother might remember something that he didn't.

"I don't know," said Elijah, "and I don't know how we got here either." Dante was suddenly terrified.
"HELLO! Is anyone there!" screamed Dante, but there was no response.
"Calm down Dante," said Elijah. "We'll figure this out."
Meanwhile, the boys had no clue that 35 feet above them Chris watched them through the camera lens with a delight that can only be described as sadistic and psychotic.
"I'm cold," said Dante.
"Come over to me, I'll keep you warm," said Elijah. Dante followed the sound of Elijah's voice until he could physically touch him, and huddled next to him on the floor of the cave. Elijah put his arm around Dante.
"Don't worry Dante, we'll figure this out. There's gotta be some way out of here," said Elijah.

Once the boys had warmed up a bit they started to feel their way around the room. They tried to climb out but it was useless. Elijah even had Dante stand up on his shoulders to try to reach the top of the hole but it was simply too high for them to get out. The walls were made of brick and were slippery so climbing was out of the question as well. They felt their way around the space and found that they were in some sort of room lined with brick walls that formed a large circle. There was no light coming in from above, not even stars. The boys figured that they were somewhere underground.

They found a hole at the base of the brick and climbed through it, but it only led to a dead end. From the perspective of the camera Chris could no

longer see them once they had crawled into the hole, but he could still hear them.
"Elijah there's no way out!" whimpered Dante.
"I know," said Elijah.

The boys crawled around in the darkness feeling along the walls of both the small side chamber and the main room but had no luck. Chris watched and almost giggled at one point when Dante tripped over a rock and fell down, hitting his head on the wall.
"OW!" yelled Dante.
"What happened?" said Elijah.
"I fell and hit my head," said Dante.
"Are you bleeding?" said Elijah.
"I don't think so, it's just a bump," said Dante.

The boys became tired after a while and curled up next to each other on the cave floor, falling asleep. Chris turned off the camera and left. He'd been there a while so he wanted to get home before anyone got too suspicious.

He returned the next day and quietly went back to where he had left the boys. When he returned and started recording again they were sitting on the floor of the room. As he went to record his foot slipped for a moment and a bit of sand fell down the hole, hitting Elijah on top of the head.
"Is someone up there?", said Elijah. Chris remained silent.
"Is someone there? Please help us!" said Elijah.
"Please let us out of here! My brother hit his head. We're scared and need help!"
Chris didn't respond. He instead watched them plead for their lives, remembering how he'd felt

when he'd been trapped in the cave by Paul and Troy so many years ago. It brought a smile to his face.

"Elijah I'm hungry!" complained Dante.

"Me too," said Elijah.

"What are we going to do?" asked Dante.

"I don't know, maybe someone will find us and help us?", said Elijah, but deep down he knew that this was most likely not going to happen.

The boys decided to crawl back into the little side chamber in order to keep warm. The space was smaller and their body heat warmed up the room more than it did in the larger space of the hole. It was about 48 degrees in the hole itself and they were hungry, thirsty, and very cold. Although Chris couldn't see them he knew that they were there, huddled together in a corner of the little chamber, trying to keep warm as they slowly started to die.

When Chris came back the next day he couldn't see the boys in the hole, nor could he hear anything. He thought that they might be dead already. He threw a rock down the hole making sure it would hit the brick wall to make some noise. Still no sound coming from the hole. Chris became curious and lowered himself down with a rope, bringing the camera with him. He didn't use any light to do this and fumbled around in the darkness for a while only able to see with his night vision goggles to get down there, not wanting the boys to see a light. He stuck his head through the hole in the wall and found the two boys huddled together against the wall, they appeared to be dead. He carefully crawled in and began recording with his camera, zooming in

on their hands held together. As he got closer one of the boys, Dante, opened his eyes. Elijah was already dead and Dante nearly was, but he could see the red glow coming from the cameras recording light and managed to say "why?" to Chris.
"Because it helps me feel better," said Chris. Dante's eyes closed again and in a few moments, he was dead.

1993

Back in the garage attic Chris turned off the video and placed it back in the box. He made sure to lock the box. Sometimes reliving what he had done helped, but not today. He could feel the old feelings coming back and knew that it was time once again to perform the only task that gave him relief. Despite the risks given the knowledge that the police now had, it was time to act again and he knew it. He would have to start planning his next kidnapping. He headed down the attic steps and locked the door just as the garage door opened and his wife and stepson pulled in.

He greeted them with a wave as they pulled in. His wife gave him a hug as she got out of the car and he said "Hey Jeff," to his stepson.
"Hey Chris," said Jeff.

Jeff only knew Chris as his stepdad. He had no idea that his stepfather was the same person that had been leaving children to die in the caves for the past 10 years. He had no idea that the first body that he and Tony had found was Chris' first victim, or that Chris had been kidnapping children for years under his nose. All Jeff knew of Chris was that he was a nice guy who had taken care of him for many years. Chris had even been cool the one time that he had busted Jeff for weed. Jeff had no idea that he was living under the same roof as a monster. The same monster that he had been trying to help Ron Clark apprehend.

Chapter 9

　　　Chris already knew of the cave that he was going to use for his next kidnapping, but he hadn't been there in years. His first task was to revisit this cave in the nature park and see if it was still accessible. If it wasn't he'd have to dig it out or find another way in.

　　　The nature park was located near downtown on the west side of Saint Paul. Chris had already been asked to go take a look there as the park board had heard that there were homeless people camping in the park that needed to be asked to move on. It was a convenient recon mission for him. He went into the park and took note that indeed there were homeless people with tents set up in the park. He would later report this to his superiors and they would send the police in to get them out, but not before he had a chance to check out the old cave.

　　　In order to get to the cave, he had to go deep into the park, and cross a stream about 6 feet wide. The cave entrance was up a hill about 15 feet. When he got to the top he was relieved that the entrance was still there, but found that when he entered the cave that the main passage had collapsed. He would have to dig about 10 feet into the side of the tunnel to access the main part of the cave. He knew this from memory.

He went back to his work truck and grabbed a shovel. This would be perfect once he had gotten a new tunnel open. Since the cave had collapsed he was sure that no one would be going in there and probably hadn't for years due to the fact that there was nothing to see but a short tunnel that had collapsed. It took him all day to dig out a little tunnel that was only about a foot and a half wide and maybe two feet tall. The tunnel was about 10 feet in length, but his work was not in vain. After about 10 feet of digging through the sandstone he hit an opening on the other side which opened up to a gigantic and glorious cave. He could tell that it hadn't been accessed in years and probably wouldn't be any time soon.

The cave was not as large as some of the ones that he had used in the past but it was well hidden and would serve his purposes. It mainly consisted of one long tunnel that had several other long tunnels leading off from it, each eventually leading to a dead end. It was a small enough cave that despite going back hundreds if not thousands of feet, he thought that he might have to stay in the cave with his next set of victims to make sure that they didn't escape. He'd have to come up with some sort of excuse to avoid suspicion from his wife and Jeff as well, as he might need to stay in there for a few days. This didn't worry him though. He was sure that he'd come up with something. Being satisfied with the location he reported the homeless people to the police, partially because it was his job but also to get rid of the them so that they wouldn't see him when he brought in his next victims.

The next step was to find his victims, always the hardest part. It used to be easy for him in the early 80's. Kids were so trusting back then and it was easy enough for Chris to coax them into his car. These days however, parents had become more careful and were teaching their kids to stay away from strangers. He'd have to find some kids that he could get to know, gain their trust, and then strike when the moment was right. He'd have to find a family that was potentially new to the neighborhood if possible.

He drove home that day after checking out the cave, and looked out of his car window at the neighborhoods that he passed through looking for houses that had recently sold or that were for sale. If he was lucky a new family would move in somewhere near the nature park with kids and he could try to get to know the family and gain their trust.

Chris came home, threw his dirty clothes from his cave exploration into the hamper, and took a shower. Jeff came home from the warehouse shortly thereafter. He was heading to his bedroom upstairs but noticed a familiar smell as he walked past the hamper. He noticed that there were dirty clothes in the hamper on the top of the pile that belonged to Chris. They smelled like a cave and he noticed that there were some bits of sand on the clothes that could only be found in and around the caves. Jeff knew that neither he nor Tony had been in any caves for a few days after finding the last 4 bodies, so he knew that it wasn't his clothing as his mom had just done laundry the other day. He found this odd. He guessed that it could be possible that Chris had done some work for the park that involved going into one of the caves but he had never noticed it before nor had Chris ever talked about the caves. Maybe it was just that Jeff had been in the caves so much recently that he was more sensitive to the smell? Maybe Chris went into the caves for work all the time? It would make sense being that he worked for the park board and repaired and checked on things frequently. Maybe Chris had to check to see if entrances were sealed and report back if they weren't? Jeff guessed that it might be part of Chris' job. He decided not to worry about it and would ask Chris about it later.

      That evening Jeff's mom had to work so Jeff and Chris decided to order pizza and watch some TV. While they were sitting in front of the TV in the living room Jeff asked, "Hey Chris, were you in any of the caves earlier today? I've been in a few myself and noticed that your clothes kinda smelled like them in the hamper?"

Chris looked over at Jeff and said, "Oh, yeah I was. There were some homeless people camping out in one of them and I had to investigate it and report it to the cops. You shouldn't be going into those caves though. They're super sketchy and dangerous," said Chris.

"Oh. Okay. I was just wondering. I'll stay out of them," said Jeff knowing full well that he wouldn't.

What Chris said had made sense to Jeff. After all, Jeff had recently had a run in with a homeless person himself in a cave so it seemed reasonable. However, deep in the back of his mind his imagination wandered and he thought about the fact that the child killer that Ron was after went into caves as well. He tried to picture Chris committing these acts but he just couldn't see it. He decided that for the time being anyway that he was crazy to think that Chris could be behind the kidnappings. After all, Chris was a pretty cool dude and had never done anything to make Jeff think that he could do something like that. It was probably just a coincidence. Then again, Jeff still had some lingering suspicions despite what Chris had told him.

The next day Chris went in to work, and was assigned to check on a broken slide in one of local park playgrounds among a few other tasks. Being that he was on the prowl for his next victims, he thought that being at a playground might allow him to meet some children as well, maybe even potential victims. As he drove around doing odd jobs at the different parks he also made note of realtor signs in front of houses, especially those with "SOLD" signs on them.

He was able to repair the slide at the park with a few bolts and some minor welding, but didn't encounter any children. He was a bit discouraged by this but knew that there would be other opportunities.

On the way to another job site he saw a man in his front yard, fiddling with a power lawn mower. The man was trying to get it started but didn't appear to be having any luck. The man appeared to be in his mid-thirties, had a short flat top haircut, and an average build. Chris pulled over and yelled "won't start?" from his truck.
"Nope, it worked before we moved here but I can't seem to get it started now," said the man with the lawnmower.
"Did you just move here?" said Chris.
"Yeah, a few weeks ago," said the man.
Chris turned off the truck engine, stepped out of the vehicle, and approached the man.
"I might be able to help? I work for the parks and repair their landscaping mowers from time to time. Want me to take a look at it?" said Chris.
"Yeah, much appreciated," said the man.
"My names Frank," said Chris, making sure not to give his real name.
"John," replied the man.
      The two shook hands and Chris knelt down to take a look at the lawnmower. He checked the pull cord tension, made sure there was gas and oil, and flipped the lawnmower over to see if the blades were jammed or stuck. Everything seemed in working order. He primed the engine a few times and gave it a pull. The mower almost started but would sputter and then stop.
"I think it's your spark plug that's bad," said Chris. "Hang on, I think I have one that might work in my truck."

Chris went to the truck and dug around until he found a spark plug that would fit. He grabbed a few tools as well and went back to John. As he came back to John in the front yard, two children came around from the back of the house.
"Is it broken daddy?" said one of the kids to John.
"Yes, but this is our new neighbor Frank, and he's going to help us. Frank these are my two daughters, Karen and Angie," said John.
"Well it's nice to meet you both!" said Chris with a smile on his face.

Chris couldn't have asked for a better opportunity. What better way to get to know some kids in the neighborhood than helping out their family? They would see Chris as a helpful neighbor and it would make it much easier to kidnap them having established a relationship.
"How do you fix it?" asked Angie, who was 11 years old, had dark brown naturally curly hair, and braces on her teeth.
"Well," said Chris, "if I'm correct the spark plug is bad. So all I gotta do is pull out the old one and put in this new one and then it should work!"
"Cool," said Karen, who was 8 years old, had long straight black hair that ran down to her waist, and dimples when she smiled.

Chris got down on his knees and began working on the mower, switching out the spark plug with a few twists of a wrench. Within a few minutes he had replaced the spark plug and asked John to give it a try. John gave a tug on the pull cord and it started right up.
"Wow! Thank you so much!" said John.

"Sure! No problem," said Chris.
"I live pretty close by so let me know if you need anything else."
"Thanks for helping our dad," said Karen.
"Absolutely!" said Chris, "and it was very nice to meet both of you," he added.
Chris said goodbye to John and his family and headed back to his truck. He got into his truck and drove off.

He may not have found any kids at the park, but he had a good chance of making Angie and Karen his next victims. If he played his cards right he could find another opportunity or two to connect with the family before making his move. He wouldn't make much contact, just enough to be familiar but not enough to make himself a suspect when the girls disappeared.

Chris spent the rest of the day doing other odd jobs for the parks, replacing a broken garbage can, fixing a leaky sink in a park bathroom, and fixing a baseball pitching machine at one of the parks. He was quite content at this point knowing that soon he would be able to kidnap Angie and Karen and watch them die.

He had a location to hide them in, he had established a relationship with them that would hopefully grow a little over time, and he was more or less ready except for a few small details. He'd have to watch around the cave to find the best time to bring in the children once he got them unconscious, and of course he'd have to send detective Ron Clark another letter in Green ink. Sent from far away of course.

Chris had been smart over the years in order to avoid getting caught or even giving a lead as to what he was up to. He always drove out of state to mail the letters, and when he wrote them wore latex gloves. He would make sure that the letter was written on paper that had just been purchased as well as the envelope to avoid chances of getting any DNA on it. One time he had been about to mail a letter and sneezed. He immediately threw it away and started fresh. He never licked the stamps and used a wet sponge instead.
    Chris had also been careful to kidnap children from all over the area. His first victims had lived close by, but after his first kidnapping he had decided that he was better off taking children from different areas around the city so as not to create any sort of pattern. He had taken children from different neighborhoods in both Saint Paul and Minneapolis (Saint Paul's neighboring city), as well as from the surrounding suburbs.
    He tried to use different vehicles as well just in case he was seen. Every time he was going to strike again he usually did the initial kidnapping in newly purchased or rented vehicle, then transferred the kids to his city of Saint Paul work truck so that when he was near the caves no one would suspect him. He always did this after hours so that none of his coworkers would be around to see what he was up to.
    When he took the children into the caves he would generally wear gloves as well so as not to leave any fingerprints, and would wear different

boots each time that he entered a cave so as not to leave footprints that could be traced back to him.

About the only risk he took was keeping that collection in his attic above the garage. If anyone were to find that he'd be done for sure. Luckily for Chris, his wife and stepson were very respectful of his privacy and none the wiser so he had no concerns in this regard.

Over the next few weeks, Chris began stalking Angie and Karen. He'd watch the house from afar, trying to figure out patterns of when they came and left, especially if they were alone. He'd also drive by the house occasionally when coming home from work, to make it look like this was his normal pattern. If he saw John out front he'd stop and say hello, ask how the lawnmower was running, and would take any opportunity he could to say hello to the girls so that they were more familiar and comfortable with him. He made sure to get familiar with them, but not so much as to be considered a suspect later on. He knew that letting John know who he was could be a risky move but he'd done it before with other families and never became a suspect when kids disappeared. He only said hello a few times, just enough to make sure that the girls would recognize him later but not enough to seem strange.

Stalking the children excited Chris. It was like a game for him to slowly figure out when the time would be to make his move and how he would do it. He had discovered that for the most part that the girls were rarely alone. If they went to the park they'd almost always have one of their parents or other kids from the neighborhood with them. So it wasn't going to be easy for him. He'd seen them walking in the neighborhood occasionally by themselves, but it was usually very close to home. They'd go to a neighbor's house to play but it would be just down the street, not far enough for him to justify offering them a ride without raising even the children's suspicions. He thought that he might get lucky and catch them walking alone on a rainy day, and offer the warm dry interior of his car, but there was a drought that summer and there hadn't been any major rain for weeks.

    Although Chris was excited he was also growing impatient. He wanted to get the girls into the cave and start recording their demise. He wanted new inspiration for his sketches, and he wanted the fear and anger that continued to build inside of him to subside, even if only temporarily. At home his wife and Jeff had started to notice his irritability, and how he was spending more time in the attic than usual and this was not a good thing.

    Chris thought about offering to take the girls for ice cream, but realized he'd be giving himself away when they didn't return. Besides if John thought that it was strange that Chris wanted to take them on an outing it might ruin his chances and affect the relationship that he had built in order to make the kidnapping possible. It was bad enough that he'd made himself known to John. This in itself could pose a risk and he wasn't willing to take any bigger ones. He'd just have to keep an eye on them and wait for the right moment.

He started distancing himself from John and his family to avoid suspicion but continued to watch for the right opportunity. If he stopped by too often John might mention him to the cops in the future and get him caught. Chris felt that he had made just enough of a connection that the girls knew him, but not enough to raise suspicion with John.

He knew at this point that it was only a matter of time before he would be able to kidnap them. He decided that it was time to write another letter. He took the usual precautions, but decided to word the letter a bit differently this time. He only wrote the letters from the privacy of his attic. The letter was written as follows:

I see you've been busy. Two more will disappear. They're still alive. You may find them, but by the time you do it will be too late.

Once he had sealed the envelope (using a sponge of course and not his own saliva) and stamped it he was ready to go. He spent several hours driving down to Madison, Wisconsin where he mailed the letter. He knew that he had at least 3-4 days before it would get to Ron and that would hopefully be enough time to find an opportunity to kidnap the girls. He told his wife and Jeff that he had to go out of town for a week to get trained in on some new landscaping mowers that would be coming in so that he knew how to use and repair them. He had actually had to do training like this before so it was a reasonable excuse to use and neither his wife nor Jeff were suspicious.

Now came the fun part. He packed up some food, water, and two video cameras and put them in the trunk of his car. He had also packed backup batteries for everything, and even a bucket and toilet paper for relieving himself. All he needed now was the right time and a bit of luck to catch the girls alone. He spent little more than a day watching them before the right opportunity came along.

Angie and Karen had gone down the street by themselves to a neighbor's house one evening. Usually when this happened they were joined by other kids and went to the park, but not this time.

From what Chris could observe from a distance when they went to the neighbor's house, the kids that Angie and Karen were looking for weren't home. The girls left the house and stood on the sidewalk for a moment. It appeared to Chris that they were having an argument. Karen was pointing in the direction of their home and saying something while Angie kept pointing towards the direction of the park. They were too far away for Chris to hear them but it appeared that Angie was trying to convince Karen to go to the park while Karen was saying that they should go back home. Eventually it appeared that Karen gave in and the two headed in the direction of the park. Maybe they were breaking the rules? It appeared to Chris that Angie had convinced Karen to go along with her and he was certain that they were heading to the park a few blocks away where he had seen them play before.

Not wanting to waste any time Chris headed to the park to await their arrival. He watched from a distance as the girls arrived at the park. He watched them play for an hour or so, and then the girls started heading home.

    Chris quickly started the car, pulled up alongside them, and offered them a ride home. The girls already knew him so it was easy to coax them into his car. He did his usual and offered them chocolate (loaded with sedatives) which they gladly took from him and soon they were fast asleep in the back of his car. It couldn't have been easier. No one had even seen him as far as he knew. Chris smiled with a devilish grin, proud of his accomplishment and all of the hard work that he had done to make the kidnapping possible. Normally he'd take the time to switch out to his work vehicle in order to avoid suspicion while at the park but he was too excited this time around to worry about it. He drove down the road and headed in the direction of the nature park.

    He got to the nature park just after sunset. Knowing that the girls were fast asleep and would be for hours, he left them in the car momentarily while he checked the park to make sure that the coast was clear. He knew that he had to act fairly quickly, as it would not be long before the girls were reported as missing and the police would be on the lookout for them. He had spent some time watching the park itself in preparation and found that there was little to no activity in the area after dark but he wanted to make sure. Seeing that no one was around, he carried the girls down to the cave one at a time, and then went back to grab his supplies. Once he got everything into the cave he set up his two cameras to record and eagerly awaited to see the girls wake up and find themselves trapped in the cave.

Chris had planned to stay in the cave this time for fear that the children might find a way out. He had prepped for this as well. If he needed to leave for any reason he had a heavy board that he could place over the small entrance that he had dug out only a few days prior so that the girls couldn't get out. He knew they'd only live a few days so he was sure that he had everything that he needed.

Chapter 10

The next day was a Saturday. Jeff slept in until around 10 AM. His mom was going to meet friends for bar BINGO and a meat raffle that day, and Chris was out of town for his training (as far as Jeff knew anyway). That allowed Jeff to have the house to himself. Tony was coming over at noon and the plan was to smoke a bit of weed, and then do some skateboarding and exploring. The two of them had recently connected with some other local explorers and were going to show them some of the locations of caves that they knew of in the area. The other explorers were going to return the favor. Jeff was excited to see what new locations these guys might show them.

Tony showed up at Jeff's house around 12:00 PM. He knocked on the door and Jeff let him in.

"Where's the family?" asked Tony.

"My mom is at bar BINGO and Chris is out of town for training. We got the place to ourselves" said Jeff.

"Nice!" said Tony.

Tony opened up his backpack and pulled out a fairly thick joint.

"Let's not waste any time then eh?" said Tony.
"Read my mind," said Jeff.

The two went up to Jeff's room and despite no parents being around decided to play it safe. Before sparking up the joint Jeff tucked some dirty clothes under the base of the door, opened the window, and turned on a fan so that the smoke would blow outward.

The two of them spent a few minutes enjoying the joint and then talked about their plans for the day. They had a little time before they would be meeting up with the other group of urban explorers so they decided to play some Nintendo and hang out.

As they sat around and played Nintendo Jeff started to tell Tony about how the other day he had noticed Chris' clothes smelling like the caves. He told Tony what Chris had said about it and Tony thought that it was a bit odd but not anything to worry about. He figured that Chris might very well need to deal with homeless people in the parks and they'd encountered a few in the caves themselves over the years (most recently the paint sniffer) so it did make sense.

That afternoon they met up with the other explorers as planned. Tony and Jeff spent some time showing their new friends where some of the caves that they knew of were located and their new friends did the same. It appeared to Tony and Jeff that these new friends of theirs knew of places that they had never seen and vice versa. Tony and Jeff mostly knew of caves along the bluffs in Saint Paul but these guys knew of ones further into the city as well as in parts of Minneapolis that they hadn't seen before.

They ran into officer Wallace once while down by the bluffs, but he had changed his tune knowing that Tony and Jeff had done so much to help Ron Clark out with his case. Basically at this point, due to their helping out the police, the local cops more or less gave them free reign for urban exploration.

Tony and Jeff didn't think about the fact that the killer was still out there and that it was possible that they might run into him. They were just happy to be exploring with new friends. Plus, they got to tell their new friends about all of their adventures with Ron. They showed them some of the places that they had explored, as well as where some of the bodies were found. At this point their job with the police was done as far as they knew so they weren't worried about breaking the confidentiality agreement that they had signed when they had started working with Ron.

All in all, it was a pretty enjoyable day. After exploring with the new guys for a few hours Tony and Jeff went back to Jeff's house to get something to eat and relax. At this point Jeff's mom was home but Chris was still gone for "training".

At the station Ron Clark was going over evidence from the case, looking for a lead that might help him catch the son of a bitch who he'd been after all of these years. He'd come across more evidence in the last month than he had ever had on the case and was starting to find a profile for how this killer worked. Now he just needed to try to figure out where and when he'd strike next. Now that all of the bodies had been identified Ron could separate them from other missing person's cases, he was able to locate where each kid had been taken from, the time of day, age, and so much more. Unfortunately, there wasn't much of a pattern except that all of the kids that had been found in the caves, were between the ages of 6 and 13 years old, and they had all been kidnapped close to or after dark. Their kidnapping locations were random, all over the city. Ron had hoped that he'd find that they were all kidnapped from the same neighborhood but he wasn't that lucky.

      He sat at his desk, mulling over everything that had been collected but there was something missing. Why caves? Sure it was a good place to hide a body but there had to be a reason. As he sat there, drinking a cup of black coffee that had long since gone cold, an officer came up with his mail and tossed it on the desk. He looked through the mail and turned pale when he saw an envelope addressed to him, written in green ink. "Oh shit", Ron thought, "here we go again". He quickly tore the envelope open and read the letter without even thinking about it:

I see you've been busy. Two more will disappear. They're still alive. You may find them, but by the time you do it will be too late.

"Not this time you piece of shit. This time I'm gonna get you, and I'm gonna find those kids alive too,"

Ron muttered to himself. He immediately grabbed the phone and began dialing.

Back at Jeff's house the phone rang. Jeff picked up the receiver and said "hello?"
"Jeff, it's Ron Clark. I need your help," said Ron.
"Yeah ok, what's up?" asked Jeff.
"Is Tony with you?" asked Ron.
"Yeah he's here," said Jeff.
"Good. Stay there. I'll be right over. This is urgent so don't go anywhere," Ron hung up the phone.
Jeff stared at the receiver for a second, somewhat surprised that Ron had hung up the phone so abruptly, and then hung the phone back up himself.
"Who was that?" asked Tony.
"Ron Clark. He said he needs our help again. He sounded kinda stressed, like he's got some kinda bee in his bonnet?" said Jeff.
"Maybe he's got new evidence or something?" said Tony.
"I dunno," said Jeff, "we'll just have to wait and see."

Ron arrived at Jeff's house about 15 minutes later. He told the boys about the new letter that he had just received. He also told the boys that the victims were still alive. He was having another officer cross reference any missing children in the last 48 hours or so to see what could be found out in terms of who went missing as well as when. In the meantime, Ron wanted the boys to take him to every cave that they could think of. Ron was going to call for backup, but not knowing where they were going or what they would find made it seem pointless until they found something, if they even found anything at all.

Ron called the station from Jeff's house before they left and learned that two girls had gone missing about a day ago. At least that was when they were reported as missing. Their names were Angie and Karen Brogan. There had been no other missing person cases reported in the last week involving children, so unless the kidnapper mailed the letter much later, these girls were still alive somewhere and probably inside of a cave.

While on the phone, Ron also told the officer that he was speaking with to get someone out to investigate all of the caves that he and the boys had previously explored. It was unlikely that the kidnapper would reuse caves where bodies had been found or near them but it was worth a shot. Ron asked that all of the caves that he knew of be searched on the off chance that the girls were hidden in them. He also contacted Hank Grady to help the officers search the caves. Once this was accomplished, Ron took the boys out to the truck and they headed out once again in search of what they hoped would be children that were still alive this time.

The three of them hopped into the truck.

"Okay guys, where haven't we been yet?" said Ron.

"There's a few spots yet, but we explored some new ones just today so we would have stumbled upon something in those," said Tony.

"I honestly only know of two that we haven't already explored with you or haven't been into recently," said Jeff.

"That'll have to do," said Ron.

The three of them headed out and explored two more caves but had no luck in finding the missing girls. Discouraged, they headed back to Jeff's house. By the time they got back it was nearly 11PM. Angie and Karen had been missing for about a day and a half at this point. Ron sat in Jeff's living room with the boys trying to come with a plan. They were at a dead end now and time was running out. Ron figured that if the killer was starving the kids as he had thought that they maybe had a day or two left to live at most.

"What if we call up those guys we were out with earlier today? Maybe they know someplace really hidden that we don't already know about?" said Tony.

"Anything would help at this point," said Jeff.

Tony went to the phone and called up one of the boys that they had met and explored with earlier in the day. He asked him if there was anywhere that they hadn't seen yet. Anywhere that might be well hidden, or rarely explored. The boy thought for a moment and mentioned that there was a cave in the middle of town in the nature park but that the entrance had been collapsed for years. No one went in there anymore because there was nothing to see. It didn't sound too hopeful to Tony, but it was worth a shot.

Chapter 11

  Chris had now been watching Karen and Angie through his night vision googles and recording them for over a day. He had two different cameras set up in different parts of the cave, and had covered up any light emanating from them with tape so that the girls wouldn't find them. When the girls would sleep Chris would crawl out of the small tunnel that he had dug out and relieve himself in the bucket if needed, eat, and rest in front of the tunnel. If he slept it was just enough, and he positioned himself so that if one of the girls found the tunnel in the darkness they would have to crawl over him to get out and he could stop them from escaping.
  He had watched with delight as the girls tried to find their way around the cave in the darkness. They were smart girls, and much like he had figured out when he was trapped in a cave by Paul and Troy all those years ago, they would find familiar bumps or crevices in the wall, or notice that one wall was wet where another was not in order to remember where they were inside of the cave. At one point they had walked right past the tunnel that

Chris had recently dug open and Chris had thought that he might have to catch them. Luckily the older girl who was leading had walked right past it without touching it.

The girls were getting weaker with each hour that passed now and it wouldn't be long before they were dead. They moved around the cave less than before, feeling weak from lack of water and food. When they finally did die Chris planned to fill the hole back in that he had dug out just a few days ago. Leaving them behind to hopefully never be found.

As he watched them he imagined Ron Clark desperately trying to find the girls throughout the caves in the area (something no one ever did for him when he was lost in a cave as Chris' parents never even reported him as missing), knowing that Ron would most likely never find this particular cave. What Chris didn't know was that Ron, Tony, and his stepson Jeff were already on their way there.

Chris continued to watch the girls from afar. They had started moving again but had gotten separated from each other somehow. Both girls were calling each other's names in the darkness, trying to find each other. This caused some issues for Chris as he had to go back and forth around the cave to try and watch both of them simultaneously. He decided to block the tunnel just in case with the heavy board.

They did eventually find each other again though, and managed to follow a tunnel that led to the far back end of the cave. At the end of this particular tunnel there were some foot holds that were dug out of the sandstone in the back wall that led to a very small tunnel that went upwards. Chris had already checked the tunnel and knew that it led to a dead end, but neither Angie nor Karen had found it yet so he watched with anticipation, hoping that they'd try to climb into it. Angie found the footholds first.

"There are little holes here like a ladder," said Angie as she felt the wall. "I'm going to try to climb them." Through some trial and error Angie was eventually able to climb up and found her way into the tunnel. She could tell by feeling that it led upwards. For the first time in over a day she had some hope.

"Karen there's a tunnel up here! It might be a way out. See if you can follow my voice and climb up here," said Angie.

"Okay," said Karen.

Karen found her way to the foot holds but wasn't tall enough to reach some of the higher ones. It was no use.

"I'm not tall enough to reach them all," said Karen.

"Okay," said Angie, "you stay there and I'll see where this leads. Don't move from where you are so that I can find you when I come back out okay?"

"Okay," said Karen reluctantly, not wanting to lose her sister in the darkness again.

Angie began climbing up the tunnel. It was quite steep and there were several spots where she lost her footing due to loose sand and nearly fell back down the narrow shaft. She crawled upward for at least fifty feet, maybe more, before the tunnel leveled out and opened into a small room. Unfortunately, after feeling her way around the room she could tell that it was a dead end and that there were no signs of daylight coming through. She turned around, discouraged, and headed back down the tunnel. It was very hard to get back down. Going up in pitch black darkness was one thing, but going down was particularly dangerous. She had to feel out in front of her with her feet to find the next foothold going down and it wasn't long before she slipped and began sliding down the tunnel in the dark, unable to stop. She screamed as she continued to slide down and put her hands out to the walls to try to stop herself but it was no use. She was going to come flying out of the tunnel and drop to the cave floor and she knew it. She could only hope that she landed safely.

  When she slid to the end of the tunnel she fell out of it, unaware that she had even come to the end of it and dropped the ten feet or so to the cave floor. She didn't land right and heard a snapping sound as her feet hit the floor of the cave unevenly. She immediately felt a sharp pain in her left ankle, and when she reached down to feel it she could tell that her foot was twisted to the right and out of place. She had broken her ankle very badly and knew that she would no longer be able to move.
"Are you okay?" said Karen from somewhere in the darkness.
"No, I think I broke my ankle," said Angie.
Karen moved over to where the sound of Angie's voice was coming from.
"Angie, are we going to die in here?" said Karen.
"I don't know," said Angie.

Both girls began to cry. Chris watched from a distance with excitement. Things were starting to get interesting. And now with Angie having a broken ankle he could sit and watch them without them moving around as much. He went and grabbed one of his cameras from another area of the cave, being careful not to make a sound as he moved it into position to view both girls and record what was happening. At this point he planned to stay there until they died. He found himself a comfortable place to sit about 40 feet away from the girls down the tunnel and watched with excitement.

Angie put her arm around Karen to comfort her despite the intense pain that she felt in her ankle. She could already tell that putting any weight on it would be impossible, and her ankle throbbed with a pulsing pain that made here wince. Karen quietly cried with her head on Angie's shoulder.
"I just wanna go home," said Karen.
"I know," said Angie, "so do I."

Ron drove with the boys to the nature park as quickly as he could, hoping that this might be the cave where the girls were hidden. He knew that there wasn't much time left if he was going to find the girls alive. They pulled up in front of the entrance to the nature park and quickly gathered up their gear. Ron checked his handgun which was in a shoulder holster to make sure it was loaded and ready to go.
Tony looked at him as he did this.
"So where are our guns?" asked Tony.
"You don't get any," said Ron.

"Yeah? What if we run into this psychopath? What do we do then? Say hello and shake his hand?" said Jeff sarcastically.
Ron reached into the bed of the truck and grabbed out 2 police batons, handing one to each boy. "Here, you can use these," said Ron.
Tony looked at Ron and said "these will do."

The three of them headed into the nature park. The entrance was a long staircase that led down into a ravine of sorts. The entire sanctuary was sort of like a big bowl surrounded by hills on all sides. At one time it had been a slum of a shanty town that was inhabited by immigrants from Europe. This was back in the late 1800's into the early 20th century. It had since all burned down due to fires. The city decided years later to make it into a nature park with several hiking paths.

As they walked down the steps Ron told the boys to keep their voices down, especially once they got to the cave. If the kidnapper was in there Ron didn't want him to know that they were coming. The three of them got to the end of the long staircase and onto the walking path.
"The dude I talked to told me to head down hill on the trail and we should find a narrow dirt path heading to the left. We follow that over a small creek and the entrance should be in the hill on the other side," said Tony.
"Sounds good, we'll follow your lead," said Ron, who had already drawn his gun in case they ran into the kidnapper along the way.

Tony led the way followed by Ron and Jeff. It wasn't long before they found the path, crossed the creek, and located the hill where the cave was located. It was dark at this point, and not wanting to give away their location with headlamps on to the kidnapper, they fumbled around in the dark for a while until they found what looked like a small hole that dropped down about 5 feet. They climbed in, hoping that this would be the place where they'd at least find the missing children, and hopefully the kidnapper as well.

    They entered into a small room shaped like a tunnel where at one end the cave had collapsed. Ron turned on his headlamp briefly to look around and noticed a heavy board against one of the walls. He moved it aside to reveal what looked like newly dug little tunnel. He peered through it, and noticed that it opened up to a larger cave on the other side. He also noticed a bucket in the corner that had urine and feces inside of it as well as a small box with some food and other provisions. Ron figured that if they found the missing children, he could use the contents of that bucket to test for DNA and catch the son of a bitch if nothing else.

"If what your friend told you is true, that no one comes around here anymore due to the cave collapse, then things have recently changed," said Ron.

"That looks like a freshly dug tunnel to me," said Jeff, "Either someone decided to reopen this cave and is living in it, or our monster is in there."

"Turn your headlamps to the emergency setting," said Tony. "That way if he's in there it'll be harder to see us coming."

"Good idea," said Jeff.

For those unaware of the emergency setting on a headlamp, some are equipped with a setting where the lamp produces a very dim red light, not much brighter than that of a recording light on the front of a video camera. It's designed to use as a failsafe. If the headlamp runs out of batteries there is usually enough power left in it to keep the red light on for a reasonable amount of time so that one can find their way home, or out of a cave or some other dark space. The emergency light is hard to see from a distance, but it also doesn't produce much light, only allowing the user to see about 3 feet in front of them in a dark space. So, while having the emergency setting on would help Ron and the boys be less noticeable, it would also make it harder for them to see in front of themselves and around them. It was a risk they were willing to take.

    The three of them crawled through the tiny tunnel and went into the main part of the cave. When they crawled out of the tunnel they found themselves in a vast wide passageway. On one side it went to a dead end, but on the other it led uphill and they could see at least two more tunnels on the other end. It was tough to tell exactly how big the space was using the emergency lights but it was at least 20 feet wide and taller than their lights could reach. If he had to guess Tony figured that the ceilings must have been at least thirty-five or forty feet high.

    Maybe it was the red lights, or maybe it was the design of the cave, but it made Jeff feel like he was in some sort of underground cathedral. They started to walk up the hill quietly. Ron pointed to the ground and stopped so that Jeff and Tony would see that there were fresh footprints. Ron knelt down for a closer look, and noted that in addition to some large boot tracks, there was also a trail of very small footprints along the wall. Two sets of little feet to be exact, and based on what Ron was seeing, they were moving together.

"They're here, I'm sure of it," whispered Ron. "From here on out watch your ass. Because if they're here, chances are our kidnapper is as well."

Ron pulled his gun from its holster. Tony and Jeff both raised their batons, ready to strike. Ron moved forward slowly and methodically up the hill with Tony and Jeff not far behind.

As they came over the top of the hill they saw two large tunnels in front of them, and another long one that led to the left and the right. It was hard to see further in any direction with the red emergency lights but the cave's design seemed familiar.

"This looks like the one we were in down by the river off of the cliff, where we met that crazy homeless guy," whispered Jeff.

"I agree, looks like a brewery cave designed like a ladder," whispered Tony.

"That would mean we're now standing in the main hallway, and these two tunnels in front of us lead off from it, my guess is to the left and right we'll find more of them," said Ron.

"Yep, that sounds about right," Said Tony.

They decided to try to the left first. They followed the main hallway for several hundred feet (passing several side tunnels along the way) until it came to a dead end. They noticed little footprints all over the place as they walked, so either someone had brought their kids in for a tour (highly unlikely) or the missing children were somewhere inside of the cave. Once they had reached the dead end of the main tunnel, they began working their way back, entering each side tunnel one at a time until it hit a dead end, and then heading back to the main hallway to pick up where they had left off. In this manner they'd be able to cover the entire cave without missing anything. The only problem was that it was very time consuming. With only the emergency lights to see with, it would take them 20 minutes or more to go down each side tunnel and back again. The light was only bright enough to see one side of the 15-foot-wide tunnels at a time, even with three of them. They'd been in there nearly an hour so far and had only gone up and down three side tunnels, and they knew that there would be a lot more to look over.

      When they got back to the main tunnel after investigating the third tunnel Ron stopped and said "we gotta find a faster way to do this. We're going to need to split up so we can cover more ground in less time."
"Easy for you to say, you've got the gun," said Tony.
"Look Tony, I know it's a risk but if we're gonna find these kids alive we have to move fast," said Ron.
"I know, don't worry about us, Jeff and I can handle ourselves, right Jeff?" said Tony.
"Yeah……sure….." said Jeff nervously. Jeff didn't like the idea of them splitting up at all but he knew that it was the only way. He also knew that it was

possible that they wouldn't find anything and have to search elsewhere. So if they didn't find the kids here, there would be even less of a chance of finding them alive and time was running out.

"Okay here's the plan," said Ron, "we'll each take one tunnel at a time off of this main one until we get to the other end. After each tunnel has been checked we'll regroup here in the main tunnel and then hit 3 more and then keep going like that until we've covered the entire cave. I'll stay in the middle tunnel each time that we do this so that I'm closer to both of you and can hopefully hear you and come running if anything goes down. Jeff you'll take the tunnel in front of me and Tony the one behind."

"Sounds good," said Jeff.

The three of them walked down the main tunnel and came to the first side tunnel.

"See ya in a few," said Tony and headed down the first tunnel, his police baton raised and ready to strike if needed.

Ron and Jeff continued forward until they came to the next side tunnel.

"Be careful, and stay alert," said Ron and headed into the next tunnel, gun raised and ready to shoot. Jeff moved forward until he came to the next tunnel and went in alone.

"Fuck me," he whispered to himself as he walked in.

Tony headed down the passage that he was assigned to by Ron. He decided to go down the right side of the tunnel first. He found it a lot harder to see with only the red emergency light to guide him. He had gotten used to much brighter lighting sources in the caves and it was difficult to see more than a few feet in front of him. At most he could see five feet in front of himself and the tunnel was too wide to see the other side. Someone could easily be lurking in the shadows on the other side of the tunnel or ahead of him and Tony would have no idea. This made him extremely nervous considering that they had already seen children's footprints on the cave floor which could very well mean that the kidnapper, killer, or whatever he was, was there as well. The killer could be 10 feet in front of Tony just waiting to strike in the darkness and Tony would have no idea what was coming. At the same time, if he turned his headlamp on to full he could be seen from hundreds of feet away which was even more risky.

    Because of the limited visibility he moved fairly slowly into the tunnel and turned around full circle several times to make sure that no one was creeping up behind him. He continued down the tunnel until he hit a sort of dead end. He breathed a sigh of relief knowing that he had walked the length of the tunnel and not run into anybody. When he got to the end he came across an old ladder that led up to a small tunnel about 12 feet up. There were children's footprints near the ladder so he thought that maybe someone was up there.

    He checked the ladder to see if it was sturdy and climbed up. He entered a small tunnel just big enough to crawl through that went upwards. As he climbed up the tunnel, it gradually became narrower and he finally got to a point where it was too small to go further. He did however think that a small child could have gotten further, so for just a moment he switched his headlamp on to full to see if there was anything or anyone further down the little tunnel. He didn't see any footprints or signs of movement on the sand floor in front of him and could see that the little tunnel dead ended another 30 feet ahead or so, so he headed back to the ladder. The tunnel was so small at this point that he had to crawl backwards for about 30 feet before he could actually turn around. He climbed back down the ladder and began heading back to the main tunnel, this time walking along the opposite wall that he had followed on the way in.

    Ron headed down his assigned passage at the same time using a similar method. He stayed close to one wall, gun drawn and aiming into the darkness ahead of him. About every 10 feet he would stop and turn around to make sure that no one had snuck up on him. He eventually came to the end of the tunnel but there was nothing there but a few old Hamm's beer cans that were rusted out and had clearly been there a very long time. He turned around and headed back down the tunnel on the opposite wall.

    Jeff headed down his tunnel as well, much in the same way that Ron and Tony had. Visibility was tough with the emergency light and just like the others, he turned around every now and then and swung his baton for fear that someone was behind him, but no one was. He got to the end of the tunnel and saw something ahead but couldn't quite make out what it was. It was some sort of object, like a table or something. When he got up close he realized that it was a trapezoid shaped table that had been hand made with some 2 by 4's and plywood. It was painted on the top as a blackjack table. There were also some old playing cards scattered on the floor. Jeff figured that maybe back in the day someone had run an illegal casino down in the cave. Although he found this interesting he had the more urgent matter of trying to find the children on his mind so he moved on. Unfortunately, there was no sign of the children or the killer, so he also headed back to the main tunnel on the opposite side of the wall, less nervous now that he knew that the tunnel was most likely empty.

Ron and the boys regrouped in the main passage after checking their respective tunnels.

"Find anything?" asked Ron.

Both boys responded with a resounding "no."

"Okay, on to the next three tunnels then I guess," said Ron.

  The three moved on down the main passage and just like before Tony went into the first tunnel that they came across, Ron the second, and Jeff the third. As Jeff approached his tunnel he noticed that he could see what he thought was an end to the main passage not far ahead. He thought that he might be entering the last tunnel, but wasn't 100% sure. If he was right though, he had a 1 in 3 chance of encountering either the missing children, the kidnapper, or both. He was scared shitless and deep down hoped that Ron would run into them instead of him. Jeff began to work his way down the tunnel as Ron and Tony did so simultaneously in their respective tunnels.

    The tunnel that Jeff had entered was much wider than the previous ones that he had entered in the cave. As he entered and walked along one wall he thought to himself that it would be very easy for someone to be hidden in the darkness in such a large space. They'd probably see Jeff coming as well. His heart rate started to speed up, and he began to sweat, clutching his police baton with a tight fist. He slowly worked his way towards the end of the tunnel, now more paranoid than ever and was constantly turning around to see if someone was sneaking up behind him. He came across a few folding chairs at one point that had been painted bright colors, remnants from partying days gone by when the cave had still been accessible. When he got to the end of the tunnel he assumed that he would hit another dead end but instead he found an opening that went to the right and into another tunnel. Jeff stopped for a moment, and tried to decide if he should head into this new tunnel or go back down the other side of the tunnel that he was already in. He turned around and looked back the way that he had come and decided that he should follow the new side tunnel and see where it went.

    When Jeff entered he noticed that the new tunnel continued further back in the same direction, going deeper into the cave. The tunnel only went one way, and Jeff decided to follow it. It was very wide, so wide in fact that he didn't see Chris hiding on the other side of the tunnel in the darkness. But Chris did see him and was already planning what to do in his mind. Chris was unable to tell in the dimness of the red headlamp that it was Jeff, but he knew that someone was coming.

Chris reached into his pocket and pulled out a pocket knife. He slowly opened the largest blade on the knife, making sure that it wouldn't make a clicking sound as it locked into place. He began slowly and quietly following Jeff with his knife drawn, making sure to stay back far enough so that Jeff couldn't see him.

Jeff walked for about 100 feet deeper into the tunnel. He had no idea that Chris was only about 15 feet behind him with a knife drawn, and despite his turning around every now and then to see if someone was behind him, he was unable to see Chris. Jeff was now well out of earshot from Ron and Tony as well so if anything happened they wouldn't be able to hear him in the back tunnel.

Jeff suddenly heard whimpering as he got close to the end of the tunnel and eventually found Angie and Karen laying there. He could tell that one of them was injured by the look of her foot. He decided to turn his headlamp on to full so that he could see a bit better. When he turned on the light he could see two girls, very much alive, huddled against the wall. One of them had broken their ankle. Jeff walked closer to see if they were okay. Chris was slowly approaching him from the darkness behind, knife drawn, unbeknownst to Jeff.

The girls covered their eyes when Jeff turned his headlamp on to full, not being used to the light it was painful and it took their eyes a few moments to adjust. Jeff breathed a sigh of relief when they moved, confirming for him that they had been the ones whimpering and were still alive. Chris carefully removed his night vision goggles in the darkness just a few feet away so as not to be blinded by Jeff's headlamp.

"I'm Jeff," said Jeff just above a whisper, "I'm here to help. Can you tell me-"

Suddenly Jeff felt a piercing pain in his lower right side, the pain came two more times and then he collapsed from the pain on the cave floor next to the girls. Chris had snuck up behind him and stabbed him three times in the back. Blood was flowing from the wounds. He looked up to see Chris standing over him.

"You?" Jeff said, surprised that he recognized the person who had just stabbed him in the back. He suddenly realized that his suspicions about Chris' clothing had been correct and that his own stepdad, Chris, was in fact the killer that he, Ron and Tony had been after in the first place. He couldn't believe it and yet here Chris was, standing over him with a bloody knife in his hand. Jeff's mind raced as he remembered the clothes that smelled like a cave in the hamper, and suddenly pictured Chris killing all of the children that Jeff had been a part of finding in the caves. It sent chills down his spine and made him feel nauseated. How could Chris, someone Jeff knew, trusted and loved turn out to be the monster that he suddenly realized stood before him?

Chris was surprised to see his own stepson looking up at him from the floor of the cave as well. He'd just stabbed his stepson 3 times in the back, something he couldn't have predicted. Chris looked at Jeff, lying on the floor of the cave, and suddenly

felt slight sense of remorse. Although he'd kidnapped and taken part in the death of 10 children, none of them had ever been anyone that he was close to and over the years he had grown quite fond of Jeff. Unfortunately, Chris had a job to do, and Jeff would just have to be a casualty of what Chris felt that he was driven to do. It was ill-fated, but Chris didn't want to get caught either.
"I told you the caves were dangerous," said Chris.

Chris knew that Jeff might not be alone and quickly disappeared into the darkness, picking up his night vision goggles along the way. He remembered that Jeff and Tony had been doing some work with a local cop (not knowing that it was Ron) and figured that at the very least Tony and the cop might be in the cave as well. He'd have to check to see if anyone else was around and take care of them as well before sealing off the cave for good if he was going to avoid getting caught. After all the years he'd spent building a relationship with Jeff, he just left him there to die.

Jeff laid there in a state of shock.
"Are you okay?" asked Angie.
"I don't know," said Jeff. He was in a lot of pain and his mind was still racing over the fact that Chris had been the one behind it all.

Jeff tried to move but the pain was so intense that he collapsed back onto the cave floor wincing and groaning in pain. Jeff instructed the girls to start calling for help and they complied immediately.

Chris began heading out of the tunnel back to the main passageway. He'd have to stay hidden in the darkness if anyone else was coming. He could hear the girls yelling for help in the distance but by the time he got close to the main passageway they were out of earshot.

Meanwhile Tony and Ron had gotten back to the main passage and were waiting for Jeff. When they didn't see him come out of the passage they figured that something might be wrong and headed into the side tunnel that Jeff had entered to look for him. They walked right past Chris who was watching them from the inside of the tunnel on the other side. Chris noticed that one of them had a gun and decided to lay low and wait for the right moment. Chris backed away from Ron and Tony, working his way to the main passage. As he was walking back however, he accidentally kicked a rock which hit the side of the tunnel making a loud smack that echoed through the chamber. As Ron and Tony were about to enter the far back tunnel where Jeff and the girls were located, Ron heard the noise and turned around. He knew right away that someone was moving behind them.

"He knows we're here now," said Ron, "turn your headlamp on to full. You go down there and see if Jeff is ok. Be careful. I'm going to see what that noise was."

"Gotcha," said Tony.

Ron headed back in the direction of the noise while Tony went into the back tunnel where Jeff and the girls were. Tony's heart was pounding as he turned his headlamp on to full. At least he could see where he was going now, but he was also visible to anyone in the cave from a long distance. He went

down the tunnel and it wasn't long before he found Jeff and the girls, hearing their cries for help. Jeff was laying on his stomach and Tony could see that he was bleeding from his lower back. He also noticed that one of the girls had a broken ankle.
"Holy shit. What happened?" said Tony.
"He stabbed me," said Jeff. "Chris stabbed me." The girls just sat there whimpering in fear.
"Chris? As in your stepdad?" said Tony, quite surprised.
"Yeah," said Jeff. "Apparently my mom married a psychopath."
Tony pulled off his shirt and began applying pressure to Jeff's wound while taking a look at Angie's broken ankle.
"Shit dude, this is a mess," said Tony. "We gotta get you guys outta here before he comes back. Ron's still looking for him. This is not good."
"How bad does it look?" said Jeff referring to his stab wounds.
"Not good," said Tony, "not good at all. Hang tight, I'm gonna step back in case Chris comes back and turn off my headlamp so that I can get the jump on him if he does. We'll get you all out of here. Don't worry."

Tony instructed Karen to take over for him, applying pressure to Jeff's wound, and told Angie not to move with her broken ankle. Tony turned off his headlamp and moved to the back wall of the tunnel, hoping he'd be able to hear Chris if he returned.

Ron quickly followed the sound back towards the main tunnel, his headlamp on to full. He could see some dust in the air as sand had been kicked up as Chris had run back out to the main passage. Ron followed and as he got back to the main passage he could make out someone running far down the passage and turning into a side tunnel but couldn't tell which tunnel that they had run into. He proceeded slowly. He now knew that wherever Tony and Jeff were that they were safe for the time being since he was now following the kidnapper. He had to catch this guy before he could escape. He began peering into the side tunnels from the main passage. He couldn't see all the way to the end of them but with his headlamp on full he could see better than before. He knew that this guy was in here somewhere, he just had to find him. He was afraid that if he went back to the entrance and waited there that the kidnapper might double back and get to both Tony and Jeff. Ron didn't even know that the children were still alive at this point. Nor did he know that Jeff had been stabbed.

  Ron proceeded forward with caution, this guy could be around any corner waiting for him and he didn't know if Chris was armed or not. He went down the tunnels, looking left and right. The beam of the headlamp was only about 6 feet wide, so although he could see better with it on full strength, there was still the possibility that Chris was hiding in the shadows up ahead.

  He went down three passages but he didn't find anything. He then came to another side tunnel and as he entered he was tackled from behind! Unlike Ron, Chris had the benefit of night vision goggles so that he could see Ron coming. This allowed him to get the drop on Ron before Ron could see him. Chris tackled Ron to the ground and stabbed him in the leg. Ron felt a sharp pain in his leg as he hit the ground. In the struggle Ron's gun had come loose from his hand and he dropped it.

    Ron fought to roll over as Chris stabbed him a second time. Ron managed to flip over and get his hand on Chris' wrist, preventing himself from getting stabbed again. He looked up and noticed that Chris was wearing night vision goggles (in the sudden struggle Chris had forgotten to take them off as he had when he snuck up on Jeff) and Ron immediately aimed the beam of his headlamp at Chris' goggles. The light was so bright in the goggles that it temporarily blinded Chris and startled him. Chris jumped back, accidentally dropping his knife. This gave Ron just enough time to break free. He quickly looked around and saw his gun about 6 feet away on the floor of the cave. He lunged for it despite the pain from his stab wounds. He almost reached it before Chris grabbed him by the ankle. Ron quickly kicked Chris in the face with his free foot, allowing him to break free and knocking off Chris' night vision goggles in the process. He reached the gun, grabbed it, and spun around. Ron was laying on the floor of the cave on his back, gun at the ready, aimed at Chris. Chris was standing over him.
"Don't move! Don't move one goddamn inch!" yelled Ron.
"So you finally found me?" said Chris, surprisingly calm.

"And I see you brought my stepson along? So that's what he and Tony were helping the police with eh?" Chris added.
"What?" said Ron, surprised by the response.
"Jeff is my stepson, I had to stab him in the back tunnel thanks to you, that's your fault," said Chris.

Ron looked at Chris somewhat perplexed by what Chris was telling him. All this time he'd been getting Jeff's help to find the kidnapper and it turned out to be Jeff's stepfather!
"Now," said Chris, "I have to end all three of you. It's unfortunate that it had to go this way, but I guess it was inevitable that eventually someone would figure it out. I'm going to leave you all behind down here, seal off the entrance, and no one will ever find you." Chris began to move towards Ron slowly. He was unarmed but this didn't seem to deter him.
"Move another inch and I shoot!" yelled Ron.
Chris smiled and suddenly jumped out of the view of Ron's headlamp and into the shadows. Ron fired 3 shots into the darkness in the direction of where Chris had jumped but couldn't be sure if he had hit him or not. The sound of the bullets echoed and resonated through the cave all the way back to where Tony, Jeff, and the girls were. Tony heard the shots and looked back down the tunnel to see if anyone was coming but without his headlamp on it was useless. He'd have to turn it on at some point.

Chris screamed as one of the bullets went through his shoulder but he was able to get away and head back toward the main passage. Ron was unable to move due to being stabbed and laid there helpless.

Chris was now walking through the cave, blind without his goggles and bleeding from a gunshot wound to the shoulder, but he'd been in there long enough to know which direction to head to his next victim. He wasn't sure if Tony was the third person that he was after but Chris did know that there were 3 of them. Jeff, Ron, and one other. Once he took the last person out he'd be home free and could seal up the cave, leaving all three of them down there along with the girls to die. He fumbled a bit in the darkness as he walked along the wall as quickly as he could, feeling his way down the main passage, just like he did when he was trapped as a kid.

Chris knew that the last tunnel was where Jeff, the girls, and Tony were. He was even pretty sure that his camera was still set up and recording everything. He figured that if he could pull this one off that the video would be one of his best ever. Maybe even better than the audio recording of Tim and Sally Hanson drowning.

He headed along the passage, coming across another side tunnel about every 15 or 20 feet. He knew that once he reached a dead end that all he had to do was double back and go into the last passage that he had come across and he'd be in the one that the girls and Jeff were in, along with Tony. He did just that, and was slowly finding his way back toward Jeff, the girls, and Tony down the far back tunnel.

In the back tunnel Tony had come up with a plan after hearing the gunshots. He didn't know if Ron had shot Chris or not, but he did know that if it

was Ron who came down the tunnel he'd make himself known, whereas Chris would not. He knew that either way one of them would come looking for him, it was just a matter of who. Tony hoped that it would be Ron but decided that he should prepare himself for the worst case scenario. Tony knew that if he set himself up right he'd be able to get the drop on Chris if he came Tony's way. Tony handed Jeff's police baton which he had found on the floor of the cave to Karen and said
"look, I know you're little, but if you hit this guy in the shins with this it's gonna hurt him really badly. The shins are on the front of his legs right here okay?" said Tony pointing to his own shin.
"Okay," said Karen, taking the baton from Tony.
"Jeff you stay there. Don't move," said Tony.
"As if I was going to," groaned Jeff still lying on his stomach in agony.
"Okay, there's one other thing I gotta do, it's a risk but I think it'll work," said Tony.
　　　　　Chris worked his way along the back tunnel of the cave, eventually finding his way to the far back side passage where Jeff, the girls, and Tony were located. As he entered and got closer to the end of the tunnel he noticed a dim red light going up the small tunnel that Angie had fallen out of and broken her ankle earlier.
"You idiot," he thought, "that's a dead end. Now I just have to wait for you to come back down." Chris slowly worked his way towards Jeff and the girls. With the red light coming from the small upper tunnel he could just barely make out their silhouettes on the side of the passage against the

203

wall. Jeff was face down on the floor, Angie sat clutching her ankle, and Karen sat next to her.

As Chris passed them Karen bravely and quickly picked up the Baton and swung it as hard as she could against Chris' shins. Chris howled on pain. Chris kicked Karen in the stomach causing her to double over in pain.

"You little bitch," Chris whispered, "I was just going to leave you to die in here but now I'm going to kill you." Chris lunged for Karen but as he did Tony stepped out of the darkness on the other side of the tunnel and bashed Chris over the head with his baton. Chris dropped to the floor, groaning in agony.

What Chris hadn't accounted for was the fact that Tony had never crawled into the small upper tunnel. He had switched his headlamp to the emergency setting and thrown it up there in order to make it appear as if he was up there while still leaving enough light to see Jeff and the girls, and enough darkness to hide in the shadows when Chris approached.

"Gotcha fucker!!!!!" screamed Tony triumphantly.
 He immediately hit Chris over the head 3 or four more times until he was sure that Chris was unconscious.

Tony grabbed Jeff's headlamp and turned it on to full.

"I'm going to go find Ron. I'll be right back," Tony said to Karen, "If this guy so much as twitches I want you to bash him over the head with that baton as hard as you can you got it?"

"I got it," said Karen, still recovering somewhat from the kick to her stomach but proud that she had managed to help Tony.

"We're going to get out of here alive, all of us," said Tony. "I just gotta find Ron, get his handcuffs, and cuff this fucker before he can do any more damage."

Tony sprinted out of the back passage in search of Ron. It was not long before he found him lying on his back in another side tunnel.

"Ron are you okay?" said Tony.

"I'll live." Said Ron.

"Give me your handcuffs. I knocked that fucker out back there but he could wake up at any moment. I wanna cuff him so he can't hurt anyone else," said Tony.

Ron handed Tony the handcuffs that were attached to his belt and said

"Here, take this as well, the safety is off so be careful, and there's only 3 bullets left," said Ron handing the gun to Tony.

"And hurry," he added.

"Got it," said Tony.

Tony rushed back to Jeff and the girls and was relieved to see that Chris was still out cold on the ground. He quickly handcuffed him.

"There," said Tony. "You ain't gonna do shit now you sick son of a bitch."

"I'm going to go get help. Stay here until I come back, I won't be long," said Tony. Before leaving he reached in his backpack and grabbed a bottle of water which he gave to Karen and instructed her to share with Angie. He figured that it would help sustain the girls enough until he got back. He also instructed Karen to apply pressure to Jeff's wound.

Before exiting the cave in search of help Tony ran back to Ron and made sure that he was okay. He gave Ron back his gun. Fortunately, both Jeff and Ron's wounds were from a 3-inch pocket knife, so although they were painful and disabling, they were not life threatening. Tony was certain he'd be back in enough time to save them all.

Jeff laid on the ground in very intense pain. Karen applied pressure to his wound to help slow the bleeding. Jeff hoped that Tony could get help in time. He knew that he was losing a lot of blood and this worried him. Jeff told Karen and Angie to keep an eye on Chris as well in case he moved. Although Chris was hand cuffed, he could still be trouble if he woke up. After doing that all Jeff could do was wait.

Tony exited the cave and ran through the nature park as fast as he could, sprinting up the long staircase until he was gasping for air. It was the middle of the night at this point and Tony went door to door in the neighborhood trying to get someone to answer. He thought if nothing else that maybe someone would call the cops on him and he could get an officer on the scene to help. No one answered their doors. Then Tony remembered that he had seen a payphone about 2 blocks away by a convenient store. He ran the two block to where it was, picked up the receiver, and dialed 911. Back in those days you didn't need to pay at a payphone when calling 911 so no money was required.
"911 what's your emergency?" said the dispatcher.

"There's 4 people trapped in a cave in the nature park near downtown! Two have been stabbed and one has a broken ankle! Please Hurry!" said Tony in a panic.

The dispatcher talked to Tony for a moment to get a better idea of the situation and then told him that help was on the way. Tony ran back to the nature park entrance to await help. He was worried that Chris might wake up and hoped that help would arrive soon.

Jeff laid on the floor of the cave. Chris's body was collapsed next to him. Since Tony had taken his headlamp when he went for help the only light that remained was the red glow from Tony's headlamp which was still up in the little tunnel behind him. There was enough light to see if Chris moved though.

"If that guy starts moving?" said Jeff to Karen, "I want you to stop tending my wound and smack him in the head as hard as you can with that baton okay?"

"Okay," said Karen.

At least this time if Karen had to hit him again she wouldn't have to worry about getting kicked. Karen watched Chris closely while keeping pressure on Jeff's would.

Ron laid on the floor in another tunnel. He had taken off his belt and tied it around his leg to use as a tourniquet. This had helped to at least slow the bleeding of one of his wounds, but he was still losing blood and knew that he'd need help soon if he was going to survive.

Tony waited at the top of the stairs outside the nature park for help to arrive. He really wanted to be in the cave guarding Jeff and the girls instead, but he knew that he was the only one who knew where the cave was and how to get into it. The police, EMT's, and fire rescue squad would need his help in locating it so he had no choice but to wait. After what seemed like an eternity the police arrived, followed shortly thereafter by an ambulance and a fire truck driven by Hank Grady. The police officers approached Tony with Hank Grady and two EMT's.

"What exactly is going on here?" asked the officer.

"Look it's a long story and we can get to that later but right now there are people in a cave down there in the park that need help!" said Tony with urgency. He continued "There are 5 people down there. Two of them have been stabbed, one kid has a broken ankle, and the other man got shot and is now handcuffed but for good reason. I can explain it all later but you guys gotta get in there and help them ASAP! You can leave the guy in cuffs for last. He's the one behind all of this. Detective Ron Clark is in there as well and has been stabbed."

"Detective Ron Clark?" said Hank.

"Yeah," said Tony, "He can tell you more about it but we gotta move now!"

"Okay kid, jus show us where," said Hank.

Tony led the team down the long staircase as quickly as he could and down to the entrance of the cave. As he led them into the cave he warned them of the small tunnel that they would have to go

through to get into the main chamber of the cave. He led them to Ron first, who was laying on his back. Ron looked up, relieved to see Tony and the rescue team. He recognized Hank immediately.
"Hey Hank, nice to see you," said Ron.
"Likewise," said Hank. "Looks like you've got yourself in a bit of a pickle here?" Hank added.
"Yeah, that's for sure. But we finally got him, he's handcuffed in the back tunnel thanks to Tony here," said Ron and pointed to Tony.
"Nice work kid," said Hank.
"Thanks," said Tony.

An EMT stayed with Ron along with one of the officers to treat Ron's wounds so that they could safely move him out of the cave. Ron explained what had happened to them as Tony led the rest of the team to the back tunnel where Jeff, Karen, and Angie were waiting along with Chris, who was still unconscious face down in the sand. Tony explained to the team that Chris was the criminal responsible for all of the deaths and kidnappings, something Hank had already known about. The team worked to treat Jeff's stab wounds as well as Angie's broken ankle before attempting to move them out of the cave.

Within an hour or 2 they managed to move everyone out of the cave and into ambulances to go to the hospital. It wasn't easy. Everyone but Karen had to be moved out on stretchers and it was challenging to get them out through the narrow tunnel that Chris had dug out a few days prior. At one point the team had considered trying to open up the tunnel a bit more but there was no time and all of them needed medical treatment.

All five of them were rushed to the hospital along with Tony who rode along in the ambulance with Jeff. Chris was given the special treatment of being confined to a room all by himself and was handcuffed to a bed with a police guard at his door. He was treated for his wounds but was most definitely under arrest.

Angie was treated for her ankle and both Karen and Angie were given Intravenous fluids and some food to help regain their strength. Jeff and Ron were both treated for their stab wounds which although painful, were not deadly. Tony stayed in a room with Ron and Jeff, and Karen and Angie's parents arrived shortly thereafter and were relieved to be reunited with their children whom they had thought they might never see again. The parents also paid a visit to Ron and the boys and thanked them for saving their children. After the parents left Ron, Tony, and Jeff sat in the room and talked about what had happened and what would happen now that Chris had been apprehended. Ron and Jeff laid in hospital beds while Tony sat in chair.
"So what's next?" asked Tony.
"Well," said Ron, "there's a lot of things that are going to happen. First and foremost, Chris is going to be charged for this kidnapping and hopefully all of the previous ones that ended in deaths, that'll drop a murder charge on him as well, and my guess is that he'll be going away for a long time. Probably for life. Sorry it turned out to be your stepdad Jeff."

"I still can't believe it," said Jeff, "all these years and neither my mom or I had any clue. "
Jeff was quite happy that they'd caught Chris in the act, but it was still very disturbing for him to know that someone he had trusted and loved could do something like that. He was still in a state of disbelief over the whole thing.
"That reminds me," said Jeff, "you need to search the attic in my garage. My guess is you're going to find some evidence up there."
"Good to know," said Ron. "I've got officers going to both your houses at the moment to let your parents know what happened. Your parents should be along shortly. Jeff, it's not going to be easy for your mom but she has to know. They'll probably need to search the house for evidence as well," he added.
"I understand," said Jeff.
"Once we've gotten all of the evidence together Chris will go on trial and I'm certain that he'll be found guilty," said Ron, "and after that my guess is that the two of you will be receiving some sort of medal or award for your help and bravery on this case. In all honesty, you guys should consider dropping that warehouse job and consider working for the police or the fire department."
Tony looked at Jeff and they both laughed, that is until Jeff realized how painful laughing was with his wounds and promptly groaned in pain.
"Our high asses? Doubtful," said Tony.
"Well," said Ron, "if you drop all that weed smoking you'd have a good shot at it especially after this experience," Ron added.

The three of them continued to chat about the case and it wasn't long before Jeff and Tony's parents arrived. Their parents were relieved to find them both ok. Jeff's mom was pretty upset to hear that Chris was the culprit and pretty annoyed that the police were searching the house, but she was more relieved that Jeff was ok.

Jeff and Tony told their parents about all of their adventures with Ron in the caves and how they had helped solve the crime. They told them about finding the girls alive and how they had managed to capture Chris with the help of Ron as well. A few days later Ron and Jeff were released from the hospital.

Jeff was able to go home and process the heavy emotional blow to his family with his mom. It would take a long time for Jeff and his mom to heal from it, but they would find a way to get through it.

Ron went back to work as soon as he was physically able to and was able to look over the evidence from the case. Between the video footage found in the cave and up in the attic at Jeff's house there was enough to put Chris away for good now and Ron was finally at peace knowing that Chris was no longer out there kidnapping children for his own sick pleasure. The trial went as Ron had thought, and Chris was given life in prison with no chance of parole despite his trying to gain the sympathy of the court by talking about his childhood and being trapped in a cave himself at one time.

Tony and Jeff were both given the medal of valor a few weeks later, and their names were all over the news for what they had done to help catch

Chris. They both found it funny that a couple of grungy skateboarding stoners were now considered heroes. They did interviews on the news and with both local and national newspapers. Their story became so popular that they even made an appearance on a few national talk shows. After the hype died down though they were no longer content to just work at the warehouse.

They both cleaned up their acts and Jeff pursued an education in order to become part of the fire and rescue squad, eventually working under the leadership of Hank Grady. Tony pursued a career in law enforcement, and eventually became Ron's partner.

The boys still took time every now and then to occasionally explore caves and find new ones, especially now that it was more or less legal for them to do so. Jeff even assisted in a few rescues when kids found themselves trapped in a cave.

Ron went back to work as a detective, continuing to try to find missing persons and solve cases all over the city with the help of his new partner Tony, once Tony had graduated from the police academy. Ron was given the congressional badge of bravery for his work on the case involving the kidnappings, and for the first time in years he cut back on his drinking and felt content with his life.

The three of them still made an effort to get together from time to time though, and would talk about their past experiences and how lucky they all were to still be alive.

Printed in Great Britain
by Amazon